Tinker, Tailor, Soldier, Die

The Mysteries of Stickleback Hollow

By C.S. Woolley

A Mightier Than the Sword UK Publication

The Mysteries in Stickleback Hollow: Tinker, Tailor, Soldier, Die

Tinker, Tailor, Soldier, Die
The Mysteries of Stickleback Hollow

By C. S. Woolley

A Mightier Than the Sword UK Publication

Paperback Edition

 The characters in this book, though named after real people, are all fictional. They are not a true representation of the people they are named for and have been created to serve the story rather than fact.

Tinker, tailor, soldier, sailor, rich man, poor man, beggar man, thief.

In loving memory of Keith

Author's Note

Thanks for taking the time to read *Tinker, Tailor, Soldier, Die,* I hope you enjoy it, there is much more to come in the series if you do!

This is the first of the Stickleback books to not feature Stickleback Hollow in the title and also the first of the books to be an actual murder mystery! I hope you enjoy the intrigue and a view inside of women's prison.

This book is dedicated to my dear, departed friend, Keith. He was a fixture at my local pub, and a great supporter of my writing - something I would do in the pub almost every day when I lived in Nottingham. So this book is for him, for all that he did to support my work and how he kept me writing.

The Characters

Lady Sarah Montgomery Baird Watson-Wentworth

The heroine

Bosworth

The butler

Mrs Bosworth

The housekeeper

Cooky

The cook

Mr Alexander Hunter

A huntsman and groundskeeper of Grangeback

Pattinson

An Akita, Alexander's hunting dog

Constable Arwyn Evans

Policeman in Stickleback Hollow

Doctor Jack Hales

The doctor in Stickleback Hollow

Stanley Baker

Son of Miss Baker

Lee Baker

Son of Miss Baker

Reverend Percy Butterfield

The vicar in Stickleback Hollow

Lord Daniel Cooper

A gentleman from Duffleton Hall

Mr Edward Christopher Egerton

Son of Wilbraham & Elizabeth

Old Woakes

A retired soldier

Miss Grace Read

Lady Sarah's Lady's Maid

Miss Millie Roy

A charwoman AKA Lady Mildred Serena Cowdrey-Smithe

Miss Elizabeth Wessex

Fiancée of Lord Daniel Cooper

Mrs Ruth Cooper

Mother of Mr Daniel Cooper

Mr Andrew Christopher

The verger

Constable Kelly

Policeman from Chester

Constable Meyers

Policeman from Chester

Constable Clewes

Policeman from Chester

Constable Cantello

Policeman from Chester

Constable McGill

Policeman from Chester

Constable McIntyre

Policeman from Chester

Edryd Evans

A welsh gentleman, farmer and father of Arwyn and Derwyn

Derwyn Evans

A welsh gentleman, brother of Arwyn, son of Edryd

Chapter 1

When friends and family are far from sight, they are never far from mind. It had been less than a year since Sarah had lost her parents and first come to live at Grangeback, and now her new family were miles away. At least she assumed they were miles away, since their sudden departure, Lady Sarah had no idea where Brigadier George Webb-Kneelingroach and Lady Szonja, Countess of Huntingdon had gone.

They were not only people of Lady Sarah's acquaintance that had left for places unknown, Miss Angela Baker, the seamstress, and Mr Henry Cartwright had left with the countess and brigadier, as well as Lord Joshua St. Vincent and Mr Callum St. Vincent.

The latter two were no real loss as far as Lady Sarah was concerned, but there seemed to be a strange atmosphere in the village since the departure of the other four.

Their departure had been sudden and heralded by

the arrival of a telegram.

URGENT STOP CHINESE DECLARED WAR STOP OPIUM SEIZED STOP ALL AGENTS RECALLED STOP ALL SAILING SUSPENDED STOP

No explanation had been offered as to why they had to leave, but their departure was not the only reason that there was a dour aether in the village and around the manor.

Miss Millie Roy and Miss Grace Read had both been kidnapped during the Grand Tournament closing ball and bonfire. No one had seen them being taken, and no one knew where they were now.

Their disappearances had not been common knowledge for a few days, but as Miss Roy was the only charwoman in the village, she was soon missed. People began to ask questions and the truth about the kidnapping had leaked into the village, along with some rather wild rumours as to why the two women had been taken.

The truth of the matter was that Miss Millie Roy was really Lady Mildred Serena Cowdrey-Smithe, the younger sister of Lady de Mandeville. She had been pressed into an arranged marriage in order to help her older sister forge a new business alliance, but she had run away rather than act as a pawn in her sister's ambitious plans.

The man she was supposed to marry was known only as Fitzwilliam, and he had been far from happy at being denied his bride. So much so that he sent men to look for Millie and bring her back, along with Grace.

Constable McIntyre and Constable Cantello of the Cheshire Constabulary had been dispatched to search for any signs of the two women and their kidnappers between Stickleback Hollow and Chester, but after two weeks of looking, they had come up empty.

The brigadier had told Sarah and Alex that with sailing suspended, Grace and Millie would be safe enough for the moment and that action would be taken upon his safe return to recover them both. However, as the weeks went by, with no word on the two girls or George's whereabouts, Lady Sarah was beginning to worry.

She was a woman of many capabilities and embodied a great number of virtues, but patience was not one of them. If there was something she felt that she could do, or should do, then she wanted to see it done as soon as possible.

Locating Millie and Grace fell into the bracket of things that Sarah felt she could do, and waiting at Grangeback for news was nothing short of torturous. Whenever she seemed to make up her mind to go searching, Mr Hunter would arrive just in time to turn her back from her chosen course.

"They could be anywhere, it is best to let the police make enquiries for the moment. They won't be harmed by the kidnappers, and George was certain they wouldn't be able to leave the country until matters in China have been settled. The village is already in turmoil and you leaving suddenly will only make the situation worse. Besides, you are used to searching Indian jungles, not the English countryside. Leave it to Arwyn and his friends," Alex would tell her gently each time, and it would be enough to placate her ladyship for several days before she would become agitated and restless again.

Constable Arwyn Evans would come to visit the manor house each day to keep Sarah informed about happenings in the village and update her on the state of affairs concerning Grace and Millie.

"Have you had any news from Chester?" Sarah asked

when Arwyn arrived that evening, and Mr Hunter had joined them both for dinner.

"No, my lady, but things have been difficult there since the Chief Constable took an indefinite leave of absence. No one has been appointed to his position yet, and there are a number of men who are trying to prove they deserve the job," Constable Evans sighed and leaned back in the armchair in the parlour.

"You don't seem to be too happy about that," Sarah observed from the other side of the fire. Pattinson, Mr Hunter's Japanese hunting dog was lying in front of the fire, half-asleep.

"No, Captain Jonnes Smith has been a strong and decisive leader since the police force was founded, but now that he is gone, there are men who have only their own interests, not the welfare of the general public, at the heart of their agendas. Conflicting orders are being given by men that believe they already have the right to order other members of the constabulary around," Constable Evans replied.

"Do you know why he's taken a leave of absence?" Mr Hunter asked as he leaned against the fireplace and studied the glowing embers in the grate.

"No, but now I think about it, he left around the same time as the brigadier and countess," Arwyn replied.

"Then he is one of their number," Alex said flatly.

“Their number?” Constable Evans frowned.

"One of the agents that have been recalled," Sarah mused as she looked between the constable and the hunter, "With so many people disappearing at the same time with no explanation and no other clues within that telegram, we can only assume that they are all agents for whatever force issued it," Lady Sarah shrugged.

“Do you think that Lady de Mandeville has anything to do with it?” Mr Hunter asked as he turned away from the fire.

“You bite your tongue, Mr Hunter," Mrs Bosworth exclaimed as she approached the trio.

“Good evening, Mrs Bosworth, have you brought news of dinner?” Alex replied with a boyish grin. Mr Hunter was the illegitimate son of the brigadier, a fact that he had only recently discovered, but he had spent his whole life growing up around Grangeback and felt more than comfortable when teasing Mrs Bosworth, the housekeeper.

"You need to mind your manners, young man," Mrs Bosworth scolded him, "You should also think better of your father than you do. He'd never work for Lady de Mandeville or drop everything to go when she called."

"Then what is all of this about?" Constable Evans asked.

"The brigadier was originally an exploration officer in India; Lieutenant Colonel Grant held the position in Wellington's army during his campaign against Napoleon," Mrs Bosworth replied.

"What does being an exploration officer have to do with being summoned by a telegram?" Mr Hunter asked with a frown.

"Exploration officers aren't simply there to find out where the enemy army is, search the land for campsites or whatever it is you might imagine exploration to involve," Lady Sarah said slowly.

"Then, what do exploration officers do?" Constable Evans asked.

"They are spies or rather the master of spies for their commanding officer. I imagine that in business, spies are essential to keeping ahead of your rivals and that there are a wide range of people and professions that spies undertake to gather required information," Sarah explained.

"Then, the brigadier is a spy who has been called to help with the war in China?" Alex asked.

"The brigadier, the countess, Mrs Baker, Henry Cartwright, the Chief Constable and most of Lady de Mandeville's network to name but a few," Mrs Bosworth replied grumpily.

"I am sorry, Mrs Bosworth, I didn't mean to imply that my father would be at Lady de Mandeville's beck and call, especially after everything that has happened in the last year," Mr Hunter apologised with as much sincerity as he could muster.

"You should be sorry! Dinner will be served in half an hour, my lady. Whether you invite your guests to stay is entirely up to you," Mrs Bosworth said as she glared at Mr Hunter, turned on her heel and marched from the room.

When the doors had closed behind her, Mr Hunter began to laugh,

"She's a good sport really. But that still leaves us with the problem of what to do about Millie and Grace, and what on earth we are going to do with Stanley and Lee

Baker."

"Surely Stanley and Lee are perfectly suited to running errands for Cooky and sleeping in the spare rooms in the east wing," Constable Evans smiled at the hunter.

Arwyn knew that the two sons of Miss Baker had been brought to Grangeback when their mother had departed so that they would be taken care of in her absence. The constable also knew that they had both been annoying Mr Hunter every minute of every day by following him around instead of helping Cooky in the kitchen.

"They're perfectly suited to ruining my hunting," Alex replied dryly.

"As far as Millie and Grace are concerned, we have to leave their fate in the hands of the constabulary until we have at least heard something from George. I will see what I can do about Stanley and Lee following you around. Maybe there is some work in the stables they can help with, or I might be able to send them to help Doctor Hales or Wilson for a few days a week," Lady Sarah mused.

"Well, that will have to do, and as you haven't asked either of us to leave, we should go through to the dining room and show Mrs Bosworth we are ready for dinner –

whether she is or not," Mr Hunter smiled and offered Sarah his arm.

Chapter 2

After dinner, Mr Hunter collected Pattinson from in front of the fire and made his way down the drive with Constable Evans.

The two men didn't talk much as they walked, but as they came to the part of the road where Arwyn would turn into the village and Alex would carry on to the lodge, Alex stopped and took a deep breath.

"There is something I need to do," Mr Hunter said slowly as Arwyn stopped and looked at his friend with a worried expression on his face.

"What is it?" Constable Evans frowned.

"There's someone I need to find, it means leaving for a few weeks," Mr Hunter sighed.

"You're not going to look for Millie and Grace, are you?" Arwyn asked with a wry expression on his face.

"No, and I know that me going to look for someone when I have repeatedly made Sarah stay at home is somewhat hypocritical, but I need to find Harry Taylor,"

Alex replied as he ran his fingers through his hair.

"And upon finding you have gone, you expect Lady Sarah to stay?" Constable Evans asked with surprise.

"She has responsibilities here that she must stay for, I don't. At least not yet. Doctor Hales and Mrs Bosworth will convince her to remain; they will understand what she will not," Mr Hunter sighed more heavily than before.

"So you are resolved to go? What possible need is there to follow Mr Taylor now?" Arwyn frowned. It was completely out of character for Mr Hunter to talk about taking such rash action.

He was normally a careful man that did his best to avoid contact with others whenever possible. This had led to much mistrust amongst the villagers of Stickleback Hollow, but with Lady Sarah's influence and obvious favour of the man, that opinion had been changed.

Since the arrival of her ladyship, Mr Hunter was a much more outgoing person than he had been before and seemed a lot more comfortable in the manor house.

Though it was a welcome change, Constable Evans had found it quite puzzling. There had been precious little time of peace and happiness since the pair had first met –

from robbery to kidnappings and men wrongfully accused of crimes, the young lady and the hunter had been flung into a world of mysteries that neither should have ever had to explore.

Yet, they had taken to the intrigues of Lady de Mandeville with relative ease, and it had strengthened the bond of friendship between them. Constable Evans had been glad of the assistance of both Alex and Sarah in many of the matters that had been thrown into his path, but mostly he had been pleased that Mr Hunter had found a woman that he treated as an equal and treated him thusly in return.

It was not a common thing to see in most marriages, but all those that Arwyn knew who were happily married seemed to find joy in the parity of their relationships. It was not an obvious thing, but a matter of respect that led to each carving out their own roles in life together, able to comfort and support one another.

They could celebrate their successes, acknowledge their separate strengths and cover each other's weaknesses. The constable didn't understand why only a precious few managed to find this single truth and was even more flummoxed that the principle was not applied to every aspect of society.

"There are questions I need to ask him, and if he has left the country, then there is also a chance that Millie and Grace have gone as well. When I have discovered where he is and find the answers I need, then I can return," Alex said firmly, his mind was indeed made up.

"How long will you be gone?" Arwyn asked with a heavy heart. He knew there was nothing he could say to convince the hunter to remain.

He assumed that this was not merely a quest for knowledge that Mr Hunter was undertaking, it was understanding that he was seeking.

At school, Mr Hunter had been the target of all the bullies, one of which had been Mr Taylor. This had changed when they had grown into adults, and Mr Hunter had rescued a group of the men that had bullied him at school from the clutches of a number of very unsavoury characters in the city of Chester.

Once an outcast, the man had become very well respected and even counted as a friend by those who had once hated him for his position of low birth and his audacity to attend school with them.

Mr Hunter had never commented on any of this to the constable, but rumours and gossip were rife on the subject, especially since the hunter had spent so much time in the company of Lady Sarah.

Arwyn knew that although Alex appeared to be indifferent to the opinions others held of him, it meant a great deal to him that he was respected and counted as a friend by men like Harry Taylor.

When Harry had been revealed as a villain in the employ of their enemy, it had hurt Mr Hunter a great deal. It had hurt him further when he discovered the true nature of the man. Mr Taylor had taken the pocket watch that Lady Carol-Ann had searched for for so long, and was now attempting to spirit it back to her in India.

Harry was unaware that it was not the watch that the duchess required, but a small silver key that had been hidden amongst the works of the watch. He was equally oblivious to the fact that the silver key was no longer in the watch, but was now in the possession of Mr Hunter.

Though he owed the man nothing, Mr Hunter wanted to talk to him once more. If he was truly not the man that Alex had thought him to be, then he would let Harry return to Lady Carol-Ann and face the consequences of his failure.

It was not an objective that he felt wise to tell anyone else of, but he did not wish to see another friend lost to him if it could be prevented.

"I don't know, but I hope I will not be too long. There was once a time when I wouldn't have cared how long I was gone from this land and this hall, but now I can hardly bear to be parted from them," Alex smiled sadly as he cast his eyes over the landscape in the dark.

"I doubt that it is the house and rolling hills that you cannot bear to be parted from, but I will tell Lady Sarah you have gone. I will explain all, and I will keep her safe until you return," Arwyn promised as he offered his hand to the hunter.

"Thank you, Arwyn. I will set off in the morning. Be well," Mr Hunter said warmly as he shook the constable's hand.

“What if I need you to come back?” the constable asked with a worried expression on his face.

"Send word to the Devonshire Arms in Beeley. The Chatsworth groundskeeper knows how to reach me if I'm not there," Alex replied thoughtfully. Arwyn knew that were still aspects of Mr Hunter's life that he was unwilling to share with him and most of the residents of Stickleback Hollow. Knowing where to send a message, should the need arise, was enough to satisfy the constable's curiosity for now.

"Come back to us safely and soon," Constable Evans smiled, and the two men parted ways – Arwyn bound for his bed in the police house and Alex for paths unknown.

Chapter 3

Mr Hunter did not wait for the sun to rise before he left Grangeback. He took his horse, Harald, with him, but he left Pattinson in the kitchens of Grangeback to protect Lady Sarah in his absence.

Constable Evans had told Doctor Hales about Mr Hunter's departure the next morning before the two had gone to see Lady Sarah.

It had taken three hours of both Mrs Bosworth and Doctor Hales talking to Sarah to stop her from riding after Alex and bringing him back, and a further three hours to stop her from riding off in search of Millie and Grace.

In the end, it had been the expectations of the Brigadier that had convinced her to remain at Grangeback. Though her ladyship was far from happy with the arrangement, it wasn't as bad as Arwyn had been expecting.

Sarah had taken Pattinson to walk down to the village after the hours of arguing to walk off her frustration.

"Mrs Bosworth, I think that it might be a good idea if

someone came to stay in the house until Mr Hunter returns," Doctor Hales said after Lady Sarah had left the house.

"Who did you have in mind, doctor?" Mrs Bosworth asked as she tidied the parlour around where the doctor was sat. The fire was lit in the grate, but it was only a small fire. The temperature was getting warmer, and blazing fires were a waste of good wood.

The doctor gazed at the small conflagration with a brandy in one hand whilst he drummed the fingers of the other hand on the arm of the chair.

"I have a friend in Wales that has wanted to come and visit for some time. It occurs to me that he would be an ideal creature to have in the house and provide her ladyship with some company in the absence of the brigadier and his son," Doctor Hales replied.

"Do you think he will come?" Mrs Bosworth asked.

"The moment I had the idea, he probably sensed it and is already on his way here," the doctor chuckled to himself.

"Is it proper? Lady Sarah in the house all alone with a male guest that she doesn't even know?" Mrs Bosworth fussed.

"An important guest coming to the village should be welcome in at least one of the great houses of the neighbourhood," Doctor Hales shrugged.

"If you think that it is the best thing to do, I'll have one of the rooms in the west wing made up for him. When will you send word for him to come?" Mrs Bosworth asked in a terse tone that told the doctor that she thought his idea was possibly the worst idea in the world.

"I will send him a telegram today and ask him to come. He may bring his son with him and possibly his wife too," the doctor smiled at Mrs Bosworth, who glowered at him. She didn't say anything else to the doctor but left the room in a decidedly huffy manner.

Doctor Hales laughed to himself as he finished his brandy and then made his way back to the village. The walk to Stickleback Hollow from Grangeback was something that the doctor had always found refreshing, but it was something that he was unable to manage on a regular basis now.

In the summer months it was warm enough for him to take his time and stroll between the manor and the village on dry days, but the rest of the time it was necessary for him to take his carriage.

The distance coupled with the terrain around the grounds made it something that was quite hazardous for an ageing physician to attempt to tackle in anything but the driest and brightest of conditions.

It was mid-afternoon by the time the doctor sent his telegram to Wales. An hour later, a reply was received.

DELIGHTED TO COME STOP ARRIVE IN TWO DAYS STOP DERWYN ACCOMPANYING STOP BRAITH VISITING IFANNA AND CLEDWYN STOP EDRYD

There was no need for Doctor Hales to go back to Grangeback with the message as there would be someone in the village that would be going to the manor at some point during the day that could take the telegram for him.

It was best not to disturb Mrs Bosworth twice in one day, especially over a matter that had already caused her to stomp from a room.

Besides, Doctor Hales knew that there was another person that needed to be informed about the Welsh visitors to the village. The doctor walked to Wilson's inn to see whether Cooky or one of the footmen from Grangeback were there to take the telegram to Mrs Bosworth.

He was sure that the housekeeper would tell Lady Sarah about the house guests and their presence would be a good enough distraction for the young lady until Mr Hunter returned. After all, even if she did convince herself that she should go after him, or Mille and Grace, the addition of guests to the household would force her to stay.

A pair of footmen were in Wilson's inn, so the doctor handed over the telegram for delivery to the household, and with the telegram dispatched, Jack could go in search of Constable Evans.

Arwyn was sat on one of the metal benches that had been placed around the edge of the village green. The green was deserted as it had begun to rain. It wasn't a heavy downpour, but it was enough to discourage most from lingering in the open air.

"Speaking as your physician, you shouldn't sit for too long in the rain; you'll catch a cold," the doctor said as he settled himself on the damp bench next to the constable.

"I'll keep that in mind, doctor," Constable Evans replied.

“What thoughts are causing you to brave the elements in such a manner?” Jack asked as he looked over the village green. It had always been a tranquil place, though it was less so when the Reverend Percy Butterfield and other village residents were shouting at players during cricket matches.

"Things are changing," Arwyn sighed.

"As they are apt to. Time marches on and with it comes change, revolution, invention, industry and no matter how much we wish that we could control the passage of time to keep things as we wish them to be, all we achieve is creating our own misery," Doctor Hales smiled.

"Ever since Lady Sarah arrived here, things have been changing rapidly," Arwyn shook his head and cast his eyes to the ground.

"A catalyst of change she may be, but it is not her fault that events have unfolded in such a manner. I am surprised that you don't find life to be infinitely more interesting now that her ladyship is living here," Jack chuckled to himself.

"You sound like I should be happy that such big changes have been happening," the constable looked at the doctor with a frown.

"Before she arrived you were terribly bored and thinking about going back to Wales. Since Lady Sarah has been a resident in our own corner of paradise, you have had to deal with dreary village matters, but they have been punctuated with things that are rather beyond any of us to comprehend. They have stopped your boredom and even helped you to appreciate the smaller things in life far more than you ever would have before," Jack patted Arwyn on the shoulder.

The two men sat in silence for a few minutes as the fall of rain steadily increased.

"Come, my boy, let us go in search of a warm fire," Doctor Hales said finally as he stood up from the bench.

"That is an excellent idea. What did you want to talk to me about?" Arwyn asked as he stood up, and the two men started to walk in the direction of the police house.

“Who said I did?” Jack asked innocently.

"Doctor, you don't sit in the rain simply to pass the time," Arwyn said with a grin.

“Quite so, I thought you would like to know that your father and brother will be arriving in the village in a few days. They are going to be staying at Grangeback; your mother is visiting your sister and her husband so she won't be with them. How long has it been since you last heard from them?" the doctor asked in a soft voice.

"A few years. I know that you have watched over me as a favour to my father, but after what happened at Ifanna's wedding, I didn't think that they would want to see me again," Arwyn admitted.

"Your father has never stopped loving you, but it is not my place to speak of how he feels over what happened. I would suggest that you take the opportunity to make your peace with both Edryd and Derwyn whilst they are here though. Now it is time for me to wish you a good day, I have letters to write to my sons and no doubt patients to see," Doctor Hales tipped his hat to the constable and took the road towards his home. Arwyn stood for a moment and watched the retreating back of the doctor.

Things certainly are changing, he thought to himself before he pulled his cloak tighter about his shoulders and trudged back to the police house.

Chapter 4

The rain had begun to fall in sheets by the time Constable Evans arrived back at the police house. As he stepped through the door, Arwyn took his cloak from his shoulders and hung it to dry by the fire.

He made sure that the wooden clothes horse was set at a height that let his cloak hang close enough to the fire to dry, but not close enough for it to catch fire. In most homes, the clothes horse would have been hoisted towards the ceiling to keep the cloak out of the way, but as Arwyn was on his own in the police house, there was no need to do so.

He sighed as he walked into the kitchen, placed the kettle on the crane and swung it over the fire. Unlike Grangeback where the cast iron range allowed Cooky to prepare meals for the household, Constable Evans had to cook over his open fire.

The water was soon boiling, and he busied himself, making a pot of tea to help get rid of the cold that had seeped into his bones with the rain.

On his walk home alone, he had thought about how he felt about his father and brother coming to Stickleback Hollow and hadn't been able to arrive at any conclusion.

His father was a Welsh farmer that came from a family that had made an awful lot of money raising sheep and heavy horses. Doctor Jack Hales had met Edryd Evans at a horse fair when they were both little more than boys, and the two had become good friends over the years.

The pair had met long before Edryd was married and long before either man had children. As the years had gone by, the two men had remained in touch, but their families were hardly as close as the pair had been in their youth.

When Arwyn had wanted to leave Wales and come to England to find work, Edryd had been heartbroken. He had always imagined that Derwyn would take over the heavy horse breeding and that Arwyn would look after the sheep farming.

There had been a lot of arguments in the Evans homestead about Arwyn wanting to leave, until one day he was gone. The now constable hadn't believed that his father would ever agree to let him leave, so he had gone without so much as a goodbye. It wasn't a sudden decision that he had come to though.

Arwyn's sister, Ifanna, had married a man name Cledwyn, a man that was heavily involved in the Chartist movement, and someone that Arwyn hated from the moment they had met. There was no doubt in Arwyn's mind that Cledwyn had only married Ifanna for the money she would inherit and the dowry that she brought with her.

It was at the wedding reception when Arwyn had warned the groom that he would do everything he could to make sure that Cledwyn never got any share of the Evans family fortune that had finally convinced the constable to leave.

His father had overheard what Arwyn was saying, and Edryd had told his son, in a drunken rage, what an embarrassment he was to the family.

Three days later, Arwyn left.

He didn't know where to go or how to even go about finding a job. Doctor Hales had sent out men to search for Arwyn crossing the border after Edryd had sent a telegram to the doctor begging him to find and help his son.

It had taken the men searching the border three days

to find Arwyn. He was hungry and tired but otherwise unharmed. The men had taken him back to Doctor Hales' house where he was fed and slept for a few days.

Jack sent Edryd a telegram telling him that his son was safe and that Doctor Hales would send Arwyn back home in his carriage, but Edryd had told him not to.

Instead, the farmer had asked the doctor to help his son find somewhere to live and a job since Arwyn had been so desperate to leave Wales and the family spread.

It was a few years before the police had been formed, but the Bow Street Runners had always fascinated the young Welsh man, so Jack had arranged for him to move to Chester to take a job as a night watchman.

When the Cheshire Constabulary was founded, and the headquarters were established at 4 Seller Street, Chester, Arwyn had been made into a constable and sent to Stickleback Hollow to look after the village inhabitants along with Constable Mitchell. Constable Mitchell was an older man who had died after the first winter and never been replaced.

The Captain Jonnes Smith had spoken with the local landowners, but Stickleback Hollow was such a peaceful and isolated place that it was agreed that Constable Arwyn Evans efforts to maintain law and order were more than enough.

Arwyn hadn't spoken to any of his family since the night he ran away, and now they were coming to Grangeback. It would be easy enough to avoid calling at the manor house during their visit, but in the village, he couldn't hide.

He didn't feel ashamed of himself for wanting to forge his own path, nor about the manner of his leaving home. But the last thing that the constable wanted was to face another argument about his selfishness and what was owed to his family and his country.

As he poured the hot water out of the kettle and over the tea leaves in the pot, his mind was so immersed in the business of imagining the terrible conversations he was going to be subjected to over the coming weeks he didn't hear the knock at his front door.

The Reverend Percy Butterfield didn't intend to creep into the police house and terrify Constable Evans into throwing hot water over the floor, but when a man is deep in thought a herd of elephants passing by would go unnoticed.

The gentle tap on the shoulder that the reverend gave the constable was met with a shriek of surprise and the kettle being dropped onto the floor, the cast iron cracking the tile it bounced off and spraying its contents all over the floor.

"Reverend!" Constable Evans stammered as he clutched his chest. His heart was going like the clappers as Arwyn laid eyes on the rather apologetic clergyman.

"I am so sorry, constable, I did knock several times, but there was no answer. I will send over the parish secretary to look at replacing that tile for you," Percy said as Arwyn picked up the kettle from the floor. Aside from the water and the broken tile, there was no real harm done, and the kettle was still intact.

"What can I do for you, reverend?" the young policeman asked as he went to collect the mop from the cupboard under the stairs and set to work clearing up the unexpected flood.

"I wondered if you would be kind enough to come with me to see Old Woakes. I'm extremely worried about him. He wasn't in church on Sunday, and no one has seen him around the village since last Friday," Reverend Butterfield explained as he wrung his hands together.

Though he was somewhat single-minded in his passions, he was not a callous or ignorant man. He felt responsible for accidents, most of which had almost nothing to do with him and even when apologies had been made and forgiveness offered, he would feel guilty for days afterwards.

It was something that could get very wearing as far as Constable Evans was concerned, but he knew that the reverend was not doing it to annoy him.

"Have you tried to call on him already?" Arwyn asked as he cleared up the worst of the spilt water. He left the mop head hanging over the sink as he turned back to look at the clergyman.

"I have indeed, I knocked several times, but there was no answer," Percy replied.

"Alright then, let me get my cloak," Arwyn sighed.

The idea of going out into the rain again without even having had a moment to enjoy a sip of tea was not an appealing one, but the constable did it anyway.

The rain had eased slightly as the two men made their way to the end of the lane where Old Woakes' cottage lay. Arwyn's helmet kept his head dry, but his cloak was damp, and the April weather was far from warm.

The pair arrived at the cottage door, and everything appeared to be quiet. Arwyn banged on the door as hard as he could and then listened for any sound of life coming from within.

There was nothing, so he banged on the door a second time. Still nothing. The reverend stood next to the constable looking more and more worried about where Old Woakes was. Arwyn left the reverend standing by the door just in case Old Woakes came to answer it, then he moved around the side of the house and tried to see if he could see anything through the windows.

Every window he reached and peered through showed nothing seemed out of place until he reached the backdoor of the cottage.

"Reverend, come here," Arwyn called out, and he waited for Percy Butterfield to join him. The backdoor was splintered around the lock where someone had forced it open, and there were footprints in the mud around the doorstep.

“What is it?” the reverend asked.

"I want you to wait here for me. Don't let anyone else come through the door," Arwyn said as he slowly pushed open the door and stepped into the home of Old Woakes.

Old Woakes' cottage was quite possibly the best kept cottage in all of Stickleback Hollow; though it looked shabby from the outside. It was the old man's pride and joy, and all he had left in the world since his wife and sons had all died.

Arwyn made his way through the impeccably kept kitchen to the small front sitting room where nothing seemed to be out of place, but there was a smell that didn't belong in the fastidiously tided home of Old Woakes. There was a hamper on the table in the dining room, but other than that, there was nothing of any interest to report; at least as far as Arwyn could see.

There was no sign of anything amiss in the downstairs of the house, so Constable Evans made his way up the narrow and steep staircase to the bedroom.

The sight that he was greeted by made the young constable baulk as he pushed open the bedroom door.

Old Woakes was lying on his bed. His hands and feet were bound, and there was a piece of material tied over a cricket ball that had been forced into his mouth.

The bedsheets around his body were soaked in blood and there signs on his clothes that he had been stabbed several times.

The smell in the room was unbearable. With his hand clamped over his mouth, Arwyn rushed back down the stairs and out of the back door.

The Reverend Percy Butterfield cried out in surprise as Constable Evans barrelled past him and threw up into one of the flower beds.

"Is everything alright?" the reverend asked with concern as he moved to Arwyn's side. The colour had drained from the constable's face, and he was shaking badly as he stood up straight.

"No, it's not. I need you to send a telegram to Chester, to the police headquarters. Tell them there has been bloody murder in Stickleback Hollow," Arwyn replied.

Chapter 5

The police were quick to respond to Arwyn's telegram. Several of the constables that knew the village had come as soon as the telegram had arrived and left lesser men to argue about who was in charge. Constables Clewes, McIntyre and Cantello were the first to arrive, and Constables McGill and Meyers came on the second day.

The policemen spent two days searching Old Woakes' house for clues as to what had happened to the old man. When they were done, the house was far from tidy. Arwyn even thought that if Old Woakes had been alive, the sight of the cottage in that state would have killed him.

The murder of Old Woakes gave Constable Evans the perfect excuse to avoid meeting with his father and brother when they arrived in Chester.

Doctor Hales went to meet the coach that Edryd and Derwyn were arriving on. It reached the inn only half an hour after it was due to be there, and Jack had a hot meal of stew and dumplings waiting for both men.

The food was greeted with gratitude as it was much needed after a long coach ride.

"It is good to see you again, my friend," Doctor Hales had said as he watched Edryd and Derwyn wolf down their food.

"A visit was long overdue, and with an invitation to stay at Grangeback, I wasn't going to refuse you," Edryd mumbled between mouthfuls.

"I take it your journey was miserable," Jack chuckled to himself as he glanced around the room of the inn and looked at the sour faces of the other inhabitants of the coach.

"Completely insufferable, but I am sure your carriage will be a lot more comfortable," Edryd grinned, "I see that Arwyn didn't want to come and meet us," he said sadly, almost as an afterthought.

“I’m afraid I didn’t ask him,” Doctor Hales said tactfully, “He’s been rather busy since I told him that you were coming.”

“Oh? Is it because we were coming that he became busy or just a lucky coincidence for him?” Derwyn asked tersely.

"You haven't seen a newspaper yet then," Jack sighed as he reached into his bag and pulled out two newspapers. One of them was from the day before. The headline read:

MURDER MOST FOUL

The article below it detailed the murder of Old Woakes and how his body was found. There was a brief description of the body's condition and how Constable Evans came to find it. The rest of the article was filled with wild speculation as to what might have happened.

The second newspaper had been printed that morning and had a story that was completely contrary to the one that had been sent to press the day before.

The headline for the second paper read:

NURSERY KILLER STRIKES AGAIN

"What is the Nursery Killer?" Edryd frowned as he read through the papers.

"You've heard of the nursery rhyme, tinker, tailor, soldier, sailor, rich man, poor man, beggar man, thief?" Jack asked as he tapped his fingers on the table and lowered his voice.

"Yes, what of it?" Edryd frowned.

"The newspapers believe that someone is going around killing people that fit the pattern of the nursery rhyme and have put these killings together to fit their pattern," Doctor Hales shook his head with disbelief.

"You don't think it's possible?" Derwyn asked as his father passed him the newspapers.

"In England? I think that no Englishman would ever stoop to such degradation as to kill another human being simply because they fit a pattern that they want to observe," Jack spat and involuntarily clenched his fist.

"Have you read the story?" Derwyn asked as he glanced up from the paper.

"Not yet," the doctor admitted.

"We received a letter this morning that followed in the same vein as the previous Nursery Killer letters. *Tinker, Tailor, Soldier, Sailor, Rich man, Poor man, Beggar man, Thief, another body at your feet. Tinker slain and tailor too, now the soldier, what will you do?* Geoffrey Allen, a local tinker, was found three weeks ago outside the Mitre Inn. His head had been twisted all the way round, and his body stripped to his underwear. The tinker was well-known to the police but reportedly had no enemies.

"Matthew Thom, a tailor of some great reputation, was found dead in his shop ten days ago. His body was covered with puncture wounds, and the coroner concluded that Mr Thom had been bitten all over his body by several venomous snakes. Doctor Beardsley commented 'I haven't seen such bites since I was serving in the army in India.' The body of Mr Archibald Woakes, affectionately known as Old Woakes, we reported yesterday, was found by Constable Arwyn Evans in Woakes' home. After receiving a third letter, it is believed that Woakes is the soldier in the rhyme.

"Woakes served in the British Army as did his two sons, both of whom died serving their country. Woakes was a widower and found tied on his bed with a cricket ball forced into his mouth. His side was cut, and his blood drained. It is unknown what connection there is between each of the victims," Derwyn read.

"I see, I think we should get to Grangeback. I have a feeling that we will see Arwyn there shortly. It would be a shame if you missed seeing him," Jack said absently as he chewed his bottom lip.

Both Edryd and Derwyn were tired from their journey, so neither man was in the mood to talk on the carriage ride from Chester to Stickleback Hollow, something that Doctor Hales was glad of.

His mind was whirling after listening to Derwyn reading. There were plenty of people in Chester that were capable of twisting a man's head right around, but the practice was something that the doctor had only ever heard of being carried out by jettis in India. The venomous snakes were mentioned in the paper as something that one might find in India, and the blood-letting of Old Woakes was something that Jack assumed was an Indian practice.

There was only one person that Doctor Hales knew of that was currently close to Chester who had been to India before, and that was Lady Sarah.

It seemed a ridiculous thought that the young lady could be involved in such crimes, but the connection with India and the apparent trust that the victims had for their murderer suggested that none of them had considered their attacker a threat.

As much as he wanted to dismiss the idea from his

mind, the doctor couldn't shake it. The thought had burrowed in and was now growing as he mulled in silence.

The carriage drew up at the front of Grangeback before Jack even realised where they were. The footmen came to open the door and brought in the baggage that Edryd and Derwyn had brought with them.

"Oh, Doctor! I am so glad you're here!" Cooky sobbed as Jack entered the house.

"What is it, Cooky?" the doctor frowned.

"Go to the drawing room, you'll see!" Cooky clucked and waved her arms around in a desperate fashion.

The doctor frowned but did as he was bid. Cooky was known to fly into panics at the slightest provocation, but she was normally very good at hiding her panic around strangers.

Edryd and Derwyn were both curious about what great disaster was occurring in the drawing room that would cause the cook to beg for the doctor's aid.

Jack opened the door of the drawing room to find Lady Sarah sat on the settee with Constables Evans and Clewes stood in front of her.

Mrs Bosworth was stood behind the young lady,

glaring at the two constables with an expression that the housekeeper normally reserved for tradesmen that tried to come through the front door of the house.

Bosworth the butler stood beside his wife, his face was the same placid mask that he always wore when he was stood before guests in the house.

"This looks like a serious affair," the doctor said as he walked over and sat down beside Sarah.

"It is. The constables came to ask Lady Sarah why she was visiting Old Woakes on the day that the coroner thinks that he died," Mrs Bosworth said through gritted teeth.

She was clearly more annoyed that Arwyn was asking Lady Sarah about this when the lady had been a good friend to the Welshman.

“Mrs Bosworth, we have to ask these questions, even if it's to remove her ladyship from the list of suspects in this case," Constable Evans said as calmly as he could.

"I was taking him a hamper. He's been feeling rather sad recently about his lack of family, and I thought a hamper and some company every week would help him to feel less lonely," Lady Sarah told the two constables.

"Thank you, that's all we need to know," Arwyn said

and motioned to Constable Clewes that it was time for the pair to leave.

"How did you know I had been to visit Old Woakes? I only told Cooky about it as I needed her help with the hamper," Sarah asked as the two policemen turned to leave.

"A slip of paper was put through the letterbox of the police house telling us that you went to his house the morning that Old Woakes died," Constable Clewes replied.

Arwyn didn't say anything else as he made his way out of the drawing room and out of the house. He walked past his father and brother without acknowledging that either of them were even there.

Constable Clewes hurried after Constable Evans, not wanting to be left behind. Doctor Hales watched them go and sucked on his teeth as he thought.

"I'm sorry you had to see that gentlemen, you must be Mr Edryd Evans and Mr Derwyn Evans; a pleasure to meet you both," Sarah smiled as she swept gracefully from the settee to greet her house guests.

Watching her move and make arrangements for her guests, no one would ever have thought that the young lady had just been questioned by the police over the murder of someone that she considered a friend.

Doctor Hales stayed for dinner that night, though his mind was distracted from the polite conversation that Lady Sarah, Edryd and Derwyn were engaged in.

He took his carriage home after the meal and sat down to write a letter before he went to bed.

Dear George,

Whatever you may hear or read, don't worry. I will take care of it.

Jack

When he was done, he went out to the garden where three pigeons were sat in a cote. He took one of the birds out of the cage and attached the message to its leg in a small metal cylinder. He held the bird up in the air and let it go. He watched it fly away until it disappeared into the darkness and wondered whether the message would reach its destination or not.

Chapter 6

Constable Clewes travelled back to Chester the day after visiting with Lady Sarah. There were a lot of unanswered questions that bubbled around the constable's mind.

To him, the anonymous note didn't seem at all suspicious, but a high-born lady visiting an old soldier with a hamper to keep him company was very peculiar.

The journey back to Chester wasn't a particularly comfortable one for the constable. He knew that he was returning to Chester to report that the person who he believed to be the Nursery Killer was a titled lady of great reputation and local fame, and the thought of what his superiors might say about accusing her was causing him no small measure of discomfort.

Constable Evans had been convinced that the note was nonsense and that there was nothing strange about her ladyship visiting Old Woakes.

When the two men had arrived back at the police house, there had been a long argument between the constables Clewes, McGill, Meyers, McIntyre, Cantello and Evans about what should be done next. Arwyn was convinced that they needed to look elsewhere for the killer, but the other five constables were certain that Lady Sarah had killed Old Woakes, if not the first two Nursery Killer murder victims.

The other constables had remained in Stickleback Hollow in order to make sure that Constable Evans didn't try to get to Chester to make a contrary report. They also remained to stop Arwyn from going to Grangeback to warn Lady Sarah about what was about to happen.

It took an hour of reviewing everything that Constable Clewes knew of the three murders and how they applied to Lady Sarah for his sergeant to be convinced of her guilt.

It took a further hour of talking to other officers before a wagon was dispatched to arrest the lady. It was almost dark by the time the wagon reached Stickleback Hollow. Constable Clewes stopped to collect the other constables from the police house, and the sight of the wagon trundling through the village towards Grangeback had rumours of who was being arrested spreading like wildfire before the wagon had even reached the manor.

Arwyn refused to take part in the arrest of Lady Sarah, and he chose to stay at the police house whilst the other men went to Grangeback.

The doctor had seen Constable Clewes leave the village for Chester and had made his way to Grangeback to prepare Lady Sarah for what he was certain was about to happen.

Lady Sarah spent the day seeing to pressing matters that wouldn't be able to wait whilst she was incarcerated. She was calm and collected about the whole situation. Edryd and Derwyn did their best to help her and agreed to stay in the village to help the household until either George or Sarah returned.

Nobody in the house dared to leave it for fear that Lady Sarah wouldn't be there when they returned. By the time the wagon arrived at the manor, there was a melancholy mood hanging over Grangeback.

The constables knocked on the front door and were greeted by the sight of the whole household staff standing in the hallway. Bosworth led the five men to the drawing room where Sarah was waiting.

She was sat on a settee with her hands folded in her lap. No one else was in the room with her, and she seemed perfectly calm when she looked up from the book she was attempting to read.

"Lady Montgomery Baird Watson Wentworth, if you would be good enough to come with us," Constable Clewes said as the policemen were shown into the drawing room where Lady Sarah was waiting.

The young lady didn't say a word as she gracefully rose and followed the policemen out to the wagon. As she passed through the house with Bosworth at her side, the entire staff had formed an avenue to the front door by lining up on either side of the hall.

Each of them bowed or curtseyed to Sarah as she passed by. Cooky and Mrs Bosworth were stood on either side of the front door. Cooky was blubbering into her handkerchief, and Mrs Bosworth was staring down all five policemen with a look that would curdle whipping cream.

Doctor Hales and Edryd and Derwyn Evans were all waiting outside to say their goodbyes. Once Lady Sarah had stepped out of the house, Bosworth turned to the staff and said,

"Back to work."

Cooky ran off to the kitchens as most of the staff dispersed to go about their duties. Only Mrs Bosworth remained at the door with the same stern expression on her face.

Bosworth bowed to Lady Sarah when he was sure that the staff were all gone and said,

"Everything will keep going until you return, Milady," he said gruffly. He was not a man that enjoyed displaying emotions at the best of times but was even more uncomfortable showing how he felt in front of his betters.

"Thank you, Bosworth," Lady Sarah smiled. Edryd and Derwyn both took Lady Sarah's hand and shook it without saying a word. The two men had hardly had a chance to get to know the young lady, but they had both been impressed by how she had handled the difficult situation that she found herself in.

Doctor Hales was the last to say goodbye to Sarah.

"Be prepared, the court hearing will not be pleasant, and prison will be even worse. We will do all that we can to bring you home as soon as possible," he whispered as he held her hands and Constable McGill unlocked the door of the wagon.

Bosworth, Doctor Hales, Edryd, Mrs Bosworth and Derwyn all watched as Lady Sarah ascended into the back of the wagon followed by Constables Cantello, McIntyre and Meyers.

The sound of the door shutting and locking caused Lady Sarah to shudder, and she was glad that it was so dark in the wagon so that no one could see how scared she was.

Chapter 7

Lady Sarah wasn't taken to the police house in Stickleback Hollow. Instead, she was taken to the police headquarters in Chester.

Arwyn sat by the front window and watched for the wagon trundling by and back to the city. The idea of Lady Sarah being responsible for the murders was completely ridiculous as far as the constable was concerned.

She may have been at the centre of several intrigues, but that was hardly her fault. Arwyn might not have known the young lady for very long, but he did trust her, and she had proven herself to be a friend to everyone in the village of Stickleback Hollow. There was nothing that she had done in all the time Constable Evans had known her that would suggest that she was a petty criminal, let alone a murderess.

There was nothing for her to gain from the killings either. That was the major sticking point for the constable. He had been betrayed by people he thought he could trust before, but there had always been motivation for it. Money, revenge, simply self-satisfaction, they were all motives that he had come across, but since the first moment that Lady Sarah had become a suspect, the constable had been at a loss to what her motive could be.

The only thing that seemed plausible was that the three men in question were all in the employ of Lady de Mandeville, but Lady Sarah had shown no open hostility towards any of those she knew were working for the woman that had murdered her parents. There seemed to be little reason for her to start doing so now and to announce it with letters to newspapers.

As he spied the police wagon rolling back through the village, Arwyn couldn't help but sigh. He had a sinking feeling that there was nothing he could do to help Lady Sarah in his capacity as a policeman; at least not on his own. He watched until the police wagon had trundled out of view and then he went to his desk.

As he sat down, he took a fresh sheet of paper and began to scribble.

Hunter,

Sarah has been arrested for multiple murders. Come back at once.

Evans

There was nothing more that needed to be said. When he was happy that the ink had set on the page, he carefully folded the letter in half and then took out an envelope, which he wrapped around the letter and sealed with wax.

He wrote *Mr A Hunter, The Devonshire Arms,* on the envelope and then went in search of the Baker boys. They were young, but they would pass virtually unnoticed and could be trusted to carry the letter and to take it to the groundskeeper that Alex had mentioned.

It didn't take long for Arwyn to find the two boys. They were sat by the lake, staring out at the water. The pair had been somewhat forlorn since Mr Hunter had left and had taken to slinking off to sit by the water in silence.

When Constable Evans told the two boys what he wanted them to do, both Stanley and Lee couldn't be ready to leave quickly enough. Rather than sending them out on their own, Arwyn took them to Grangeback to find Mrs Bosworth to arrange for one of the coachmen to take them.

The constable went to the back door to avoid seeing his father and brother, he knew that Doctor Hales had invited them to Grangeback and had hoped to orchestrate some form of family reunion, but Arwyn was more concerned about the Nursery Killer and Lady Sarah than his own family.

“Oh, constable, you will make sure they take good care of my lady, won’t you?” Cooky asked as Arwyn opened the back door to the kitchen.

“I will do what I can, Cooky, but I need to see Mrs Bosworth. Stanley and Lee are carrying a message to Mr Hunter for me," Arwyn explained to the faffing cook.

"Oh, yes, he needs to know what's happened to my lady. Oh, if he were here, none of this would have happened. Why did he have to go away at a time like this? I wish he and the brigadier were here," Cooky moaned as she collapsed into her chair in the corner of the kitchen.

“What is it now, Cooky?” Mrs Bosworth asked with frustration as she bustled into the kitchen. She had spent most of the last few days dealing with Cooky howling and collapsing every hour or so, and it had worn down the housekeeper's nerves.

Mrs Bosworth didn't see Arwyn or the Baker boys until she had made her way into the kitchen proper.

"Mrs Bosworth, I came to see about a coachman to take these two boys to Beeley. They have a message for Mr Hunter," Constable Evans explained.

"Oh, is that where he's run off to then? I can certainly make sure the boys get there and back again safely. I'll have a coach made ready for them now. Did you want to come in and see your father and brother? They've been asking about you," Mrs Bosworth said as she looked over the young policeman.

"Thank you, but no. I have three murders to solve. Is Doctor Hales still here? I wanted to talk to him about Lady Sarah's solicitor," Arwyn asked.

"No, he's had to go see Miss Gunn and Miss Beaumont. They've both come down with what seems to be a nasty case of influenza. I would expect him to be back here this evening or back at his house this afternoon," Mrs Bosworth explained.

"Thank you, I'll try and see him at home. And thank

you for the coach," Constable Evans said and slipped out of the back door before Mrs Bosworth, or Cooky could say anything else to him, and before Derwyn or Edryd wandered into the kitchen.

The constable walked back to the village and made his way to the doctor's home. As he reached the top of the path to his door, Arwyn spotted the doctor making his way down the lane.

"Good afternoon, constable. I was glad to see that you had no part in the arrest of Lady Sarah earlier," the doctor smiled at Arwyn as he held out his hand in greeting.

"Did you manage to find a solicitor for her?" Constable Evans asked as he took the doctor's hand and shook it firmly.

"I did, he is coming up from London for her court hearing tomorrow, and one of his associates in Manchester is already dealing with the situation in Chester now. They will try to have her released from prison until the trial, then at the very least, she won't be stuck in a prison cell. What are you doing to prove her innocence?" Doctor Hales asked. There was an edge to his voice that told Arwyn that though the constable hadn't been there to arrest Lady Sarah, the doctor thought Arwyn should have done more to prevent it from happening.

“I have sent for Mr Hunter. I can't investigate all of this alone, especially when the constabulary is already certain that they have the Nursery Killer. If anyone finds out that I am looking for another killer, then I will not only be in danger of losing my job, but I also risk the real killer getting away with his crimes," Arwyn replied.

"And the person that is trying to frame Lady Sarah will also get away with it," the doctor sighed with resignation.

"Let the solicitors do what they can for her ladyship, I will keep investigating, but she will need all of you to be there at her hearing tomorrow," the constable said and then left the doctor to prepare for his dinner at Grangeback. Arwyn walked home to the police house and felt distinctly uneasy when he saw Constable Clewes waiting for him inside,

“What is it?” Arwyn frowned.

"The evening edition of the paper," Constable Clewes said as he handed a copy of the newly printed newspaper to Constable Evans.

Arwyn looked down at the newspaper and read it with increasing despair.

ARREST AND SCANDAL

An arrest was made earlier today in the case of the Nursery Killer. Hours before police went to make the arrest, this newspaper received another letter from the killer. Tinker, Tailor, Soldier, Sailor, Rich man, Poor man, Beggar man, Thief, another body at your feet. Tinker, tailor and soldier dead, sailor left floating – oh how he bled!

The body of Mr Brian Nash was found in the Manchester Canal this morning. He had been stabbed, and vital organs had been removed before his body was thrown into the canal. Reports issued say that he disappeared on Monday after meeting with Lady Sarah Montgomery Baird Watson-Wentworth at the Chester Cathedral. Mr Nash was a merchant sailor who had made a significant fortune importing luxury goods from India. He left his fortune to the church.

Lady Montgomery Baird Watson-Wentworth was arrested this morning by the Cheshire Constabulary after being linked to the first three victims of the Nursery Killer.

Arwyn handed the newspaper back to Constable Clewes with shaking hands.

"I know that you don't want to believe that your friend did this, but she knew the four victims. She was the last person to see at least two of them," Clewes sighed, but Constable Evans wasn't listening.

He collapsed into a chair and thought.

Chapter 8

Though Mr Harry Taylor was from Staffordshire, Alex knew that his school friend was much more comfortable in Derbyshire than he was in any other corner of the world.

My. Taylor was the youngest of all his brothers and as a result, had been somewhat expendable as far as his father was concerned. The Taylors of Staffordshire had three daughters and seven sons. The eldest son was going to inherit the family fortune and had married an appropriate woman before Harry's first birthday.

Then there were the two elder sisters, twins who were only a year younger than the heir. They were both married to men of independent means and had left home before Harry could walk.

Of the remaining brothers, one was a captain in the navy, one was a major in the rifle regiment, one was a wine merchant who spent most of his time in France finding new vineyards to import product from. Another was a bishop who was rumoured to be in good standing to be Archbishop of York one day.

The final brother was part of the household cavalry, whom no one had seen for several years. The third sister, and last member of the family, had drowned on the Serpentine when she was a child. Harry and some of his school friends had taken a boat out as part of a family trip to London to visit Lord de Mandeville and his wife.

Harry's younger sister had cried until the boys had agreed she could accompany them in the boat. The boat had been in poor condition and sorely overloaded when the boys set out, so to have it sink should not have surprised anyone.

Mr Taylor had tried in vain to reach his sister, whose dress had snagged on the rowlock, pulling her down with the boat as it sank.

The man who had rented the boat to the boys had been sent to prison for causing the young girl's death, and it had been Lord Mandeville that had ensured that the man was incarcerated to help comfort the Taylor family.

Lady de Mandeville had been the only person that had understood how Harry felt after his sister had died. She had taken the young man to Derbyshire to stay at Chatsworth House to help him deal with his grief. After that, whenever she had been in England, the countess had taken Mr Taylor to Derbyshire. It was no surprise to his parents when their son went to work for Lady de Mandeville, though they had no idea what his job entailed.

Mr Hunter didn't know about Lady de Mandeville's effect on Harry's life, but Alex knew that Harry had spent many holidays in Derbyshire and had always been a happier person when he returned from these vacations.

Alex knew many the gamekeepers and groundskeepers at the great houses across Britain, and staying at the Devonshire Arms meant that Mr Hunter could meet with Mr Foottit when the groundskeeper from Chatsworth came in for his evening drink.

If anyone was lurking around the area or strange things had been disappearing, then Mr Foottit would know.

"Good evening, Mr Hunter. Didn't expect to see you here," Mr Foottit said as he walked into the inn and saw Alex sat facing the door.

"Good evening, Mr Foottit. I'm glad to see your beard finally grew in," Alex replied with a slight smile.

"At least I can grow a beard. What brings you to the east?" Mr Foottit asked as he sat down next to Mr Hunter.

"I am looking for someone," Alex replied as the barmaid brought over a bottle of beer and placed it in front of Mr Foottit.

"And who might you be looking for?" Mr Foottit asked as he pulled the cork out of the bottle and began to drink from it.

"Harry Taylor," Alex murmured out of the corner of his mouth so that he wouldn't be overheard by anyone else in the room.

"I see; unfinished business?" Mr Foottit asked as he kept his eyes fixed straight ahead of him. If he was surprised by whom Mr Hunter was searching for, it didn't register on his face.

"Something like that," Alex admitted.

"Well, he's not at the main house, but if you're looking for a man that doesn't want to be found, I would head to the north," Mr Foottit said as he glanced over towards the bar.

"For how long?" Alex asked.

"About a day on foot. You might find a man at the

foot of a tree," Mr Foottit replied. He drained the last of the beer from the bottle and stood up from the table, "I look forward to seeing you again, Mr Hunter." the groundskeeper said before he turned and left the inn.

Alex sat at his table and carefully looked over the people in the pub. No one appeared to be watching him, but all the same, he decided to take a room for the night before he headed north.

Harald was stabled at the inn, and riding him to the north would be much faster than walking. If he set off at 6 o'clock in the morning, then he would be certain to find the gentleman he sought before the light bled from the sky.

The beds at the Devonshire Arms were very comfortable, far more comfortable than Mr Hunter was expecting them to be. He went to sleep that night and dreamed that he was back at Grangeback with Lady Sarah on his arm. It was a dream that could now be realised, or at least would be when George came back from wherever he was.

He awoke at 5 o'clock in the morning, as he always did. A bowl and a jug of water were in the room for him to wash with, which he did, before going down to the quiet of the bar below. He had paid for the room the night before and had asked for a ploughman's lunch to be packed and left for him on the bar.

He found the bundle of cheese, ham, a small jar of pickle, some bread and an apple with a skin of water waiting for him on one of the tables with a note from the barmaid.

He opened the note and read it briefly before throwing it on the fire. The morning was crisp and cool, not cold, but a good temperature for riding in. He saddled Harald and then rode to the north.

The countryside in the Derbyshire hills was beautiful. There were bridle paths and dirt tracks that wound through fields of sheep and cows. It wasn’t that different from Cheshire as far as rolling hills and green fields went, but the lands were unfamiliar to the hunter.

The sun was rising as Harald, and he left the Devonshire Arms, and with clear blue skies, it wasn't hard for him to head north.

He thought about what he was going to say to Harry when he found him, but after several hours, Alex still didn't know how he would find out what he wanted to know.

He stopped for lunch just before twelve when he

came across a brook and some long grass that Harald could feast on and slake his thirst.

There were signs along the track that Alex had followed that showed a man had passed that way and had done his best not to leave any sign of his passing. It was a skill that few men had, and Mr Hunter doubted that any of them, aside from Mr Taylor, had passed to the north of the Devonshire Arms in the last few weeks.

It was mid-afternoon when Mr Hunter rode up the track and saw a man sat at the foot of a large oak tree.

"Leave the horse there, Hunter," Harry said firmly as he stoked the small fire in front of him with a large stick.

Alex did as Harry said. He dismounted and tied Harald's reins around the low hanging branches of the closest tree.

"You don't seem surprised to see me," Alex said as he slowly walked towards where Harry was sitting.

"No, I can't say that I am surprised. But I am not sure what you hope to gain from this excursion," Mr Taylor replied thoughtfully. He didn't seem to bear Mr Hunter any malice as he sat by his fire, looking more like a vagrant than the young gentleman he was.

Alex made his way to the fire and sat down opposite Harry.

“I take it you delivered your package?” Mr Hunter said as he gazed at the flames.

"I did. Though truth be told, I would rather not have had you involved in all of this. Here," Harry said as he handed over Old Woakes' fishing rod and Miss Baker's leather tools, "These should probably go back to the people that own them. I don't need them anymore."

“And why is that?” Mr Hunter asked as he accepted the offered items.

"I will be leaving soon. There are no ships right now, but in a few weeks, there will be. My employer wants me to join her, and I doubt I will be coming back to England anytime soon," Harry replied with a tinge of sadness to his voice.

“Then you were waiting here just for me?” Mr Hunter asked.

"In part, the other part of me came to say goodbye to somewhere that I love. I may never get to see this countryside again, and I wanted to make sure that I had the image of it emblazoned on memory for what remains of my life," Mr Taylor replied, "What is it that you wanted to say to me?"

"I wanted to know if you knew what happened to Miss Read and Miss Roy," Alex said as he focused on examining the leather tools that belonged to Miss Baker.

"I doubt that's the only thing you wanted to ask me about, but I heard about Mildred being taken and Lady Sarah's maid. I doubt that you will find them unless they want to be found though. It would be a waste of energy to go looking for them; not even my employer is attempting that," Harry replied.

"So she is leaving her sister at the mercy of Fitzwilliam?" Alex asked with surprise.

"Not exactly, but I have not been charged with her recovery and nor has anyone else. Are you sure there is nothing else? You have come a long way from your home and your love; you might as well ask the question gnawing at your heart," Mr Taylor said, looking at Alex for the first time.

"Last time we met, you said that this was just business, that it wasn't personal," Alex began.

"That's right," Harry agreed.

"How can business not be personal? These are people's lives that you've been playing with," the frustration and pain that Mr Hunter had been feeling over Harry's betrayal came bubbling up inside of him as he spoke.

"When it comes to business, there are always lives caught in the middle. Those outside of business fail to understand that no matter what decisions are made, someone will always lose out. A contract is awarded to one company, and the other goes out of business, but the company with the contract takes on new employees and spends its money on local labour. As a result, the lives of those people become better. In every aspect of life, there are winners and losers. You should know that I was given permission to kill her ladyship in order to secure the package. Lord St. Vincent was convinced that it was necessary, but he left it in my hands. The truth be told, I like her. She's a good match for you, and no doubt will make life much more interesting in our drab social circle. It is a shame that Lieutenant Forsythe failed in his attempt to recover the package. If he hadn't, then you might still call me a friend. As it is, let us part ways with the thought that no matter where I go in life and what happens, I will always be your friend - whether you believe that or not is up to you," Mr Taylor said, signalling that their conversation was done.

Alex rose from beside the fire without saying another word and walked back to Harald. He put the leather tools into one of the saddlebags and strapped the fishing rod to the back of the saddle. When he was mounted, he cast one final look back at Harry.

He was still sitting at the foot of the tree, playing with the fire. Alex didn't know whether he could trust anything that Harry had said, but the thought that the young gentleman was still his friend made Alex feel slightly better about it all.

Alex had to spend the night sleeping under the stars, it wasn't a hardship for the hunter, but when it started to rain, he woke up and sheltered under a tree as best he could.

When the dawn broke, Mr Hunter made his way back to the Devonshire Arms and took a room for two days. He went to bed, and the next thing he knew, there was a fist hammering on his door.

Alex stumbled out of bed and opened the door to find Mr Foottit stood in the doorway,

"There's two lads in the bar that brought this for

you," Mr Foottit said, handing over the message from Constable Evans.

Alex opened it and read the contents with alarm. He grabbed his possessions and pushed past Mr Foottit to get down to the bar.

Stanley and Lee Baker were sat with the coachman and great smiles spread across their faces as they saw the hunter come hurtling down the stairs.

They were on the road within the hour on the way back to Grangeback. Mr Hunter rode beside the carriage as it trundled along with the two Baker boys sleeping inside.

Chapter 9

Mrs Bosworth was sat by the window, keeping watch for the carriage returning. She had let many of her duties lapse in the last few days, as had most of the household staff, but nobody seemed to mind whilst their thoughts were preoccupied with the grave matter of Lady Sarah's arrest.

Doctor Hales was sat playing cards with Edryd and Derwyn, though none of them were really concentrating on the game. Only Bosworth continued to perform his duties flawlessly; he kept busy to keep himself from worrying.

"They're here!" Mrs Bosworth's voice rang out the moment that she saw the carriage coming up the drive with Mr Hunter riding beside it. She rushed out of the front door before anyone had a chance to react to her call.

By the time that the carriage and rider had reached the front of the house, Doctor Hales, Cooky, Bosworth, Edryd and Derwyn had all joined the housekeeper on the front steps.

"What's happened?" Alex asked from Harald's back.

"Oh, Mr Hunter! It's terrible!" Cooky shrieked. Alex looked at Mrs Bosworth to explain whilst Cooky threw herself into a fit of hysterics.

"Lady Sarah was taken to court this morning for a hearing of the charges against her. She has been sent to prison pending trial for the murders of the four men that this Nursery Killer claims to have killed," Mrs Bosworth explained as calmly as she could.

"What? What killings?" Alex demanded.

"You best go see Constable Evans; he can explain all of this much better than we can," Doctor Hales said as he walked over to the carriage to help the two sleepy Baker boys out of it. Alex nodded and wheeled Harald round and headed back down to the village.

His heart was pounding in his chest as he rode. He cut across the fields and rode recklessly down the steep drop that led down to the road.

He reached Wilson's Inn and left Harald with the stable boys before running the rest of the way to the police house. He didn't stop to knock at the door but burst through it to find Constable Evans sat in his living room staring at the empty fire grate.

"What the devil has happened?" Alex demanded.

"Read the newspapers first, then I'll explain," Arwyn replied as he held out the four stories that had appeared in the press about the Nursery Killer. When he had finished, Alex turned to the constable and said,

"How can they think that Sarah is involved with any of this?"

"Because someone has gone out of their way to murder people not long after they have been seen with her ladyship. The killings have all been connected to India in some way, and there is no other suspect," Constable Evans sighed.

"You don't believe that she did this, do you?" Mr Hunter demanded hotly.

"No, I don't. That's why I sent you the note. I can't prove that she's innocent without your help," Arwyn replied.

Alex sat down beside Arwyn and listened whilst the constable told him everything that the police knew and the details that hadn't been reported in the newspapers.

When the constable was finished, he took the hunter to Old Woakes' house to look at the crime scene. No one had been in to clean the house since the body had been taken away and large muddy footprints were covering the floor of the cottage from where the policeman had been tramping through.

"Sarah brought him the hamper," Alex sighed as he walked around the cottage.

"She did, the coroner said that Old Woakes was murdered not long after she was seen coming down to him," Arwyn replied.

"It doesn't make sense though. Aside from lacking a motive, Sarah just isn't stupid enough to leave so much evidence behind," Alex tutted as he let his eyes scan every surface carefully.

He was used to looking for little details; tiny signs of something that shouldn't be. In the forest, these things told him if poachers were on the land and trying to move unseen, if there was a new predator in the woods, or if the animals' patterns of movement had changed. If animal movement patterns had changed, it could signal a poisoned water supply, people in the area that had forced them to move differently, or sickness spreading amongst the fauna and flora. Being observant was part of his job and the years he had spent honing these skills might now prove to be the difference in saving Lady Sarah's life and watching her swing from the gallows.

"One of the victims was killed by snakes," the hunter said thoughtfully, as he stood looking at the contents of the hamper.

Most of the food and drink was still inside it. Mr Hunter had helped Lady Sarah to pack the hamper and even helped her to choose things that Old Woakes would like to include in it.

Alex knew that Old Woakes preferred Elderflower wine to bottles of beer, and that pâté de foie gras would not be as appreciated as dried venison and beef biltong. The only things that Alex could tell were missing were the dried venison and the beef biltong from the hamper. The bread, the jars of preserves, the tea leaves, the Elderflower wine and the almond cake were all still in the hamper.

To begin with, Mr Hunter thought that Old Woakes may have begun to unpack the hamper before he was attacked, but a cursory search of the kitchen revealed that there was no sign of the dried meats anywhere.

It was hard to see signs of any footprints on the floor, other than those left by the police, but there were none in the small sitting room or the dining room. In fact, there were no signs that anyone had been in the sitting room or dining room apart from the marks in the doorway that had been left by Arwyn's boots.

The house had been swept clean and scrubbed. Even the cushions on the two faded armchairs had been plumped and smoothed so that it looked like no one had sat on them for years.

The beams on the roof were exceptional low so that both Alex and Arwyn had to stoop as they explored the house. The hunter made sure that he scanned every beam as he passed until he spotted some dried blood with a few strands of greasy, black hair matted into it. The beams were rough, and Alex had been caught out, once or twice, in the kitchen where he had hit his head, and some of his hair had snagged on a splinter.

"Did any of the constabulary hit their heads on the beams?" Alex asked as he squinted at the blood and hair on the beam.

“If they did, they would have been wearing their helmets, so would have done more damage to the beam than to themselves. Why? What have you found?” Constable Evans asked as he made his way over to where Mr Hunter was stooped.

"Something the killer left behind," Alex sighed and began to make his way up the stairs. The sight of the blood in the bedroom didn't faze the hunter for even a moment, but it was something that was still difficult for Constable Evans to look at.

Dealing with violent drunks and thieves is one thing, but the scent and sight of blood is quite another. It was something that took some people years to desensitise themselves to, and others were never able to smell or see it without feeling more than a little queasy.

"He was standing here," Alex frowned as he stepped around the bed to where there was a void in the blood splatter that reached across the floor and two of the walls close to the bed.

“How can you tell?” Arwyn frowned.

"The blood hit him instead of the floor and walls," Alex replied with a frown as he slowly walked around the bed. The clicked his tongue against his teeth as he thought.

When he had seen enough, Mr Hunter and Constable Evans quietly left the house and closed the door behind them. Arwyn was relieved to be out of the place. Since Old Woakes had died, the constable had felt like the house was covered in an evil curse that made the atmosphere inside the cottage far from pleasant.

Neither man said a word as they made their way down the lane and back towards the police house. Mr Hunter's brain was picking through everything that he had just seen, whereas Arwyn was glad to be out of the cottage and was enjoying the light spring breeze on his face.

When they had stepped back into the police house, and Constable Evans had filled the kettle, the two men began to talk.

"Someone went to a lot of trouble to remove all signs they had been in the house. Even when Old Woakes kept the cottage tidy, it was never as clean as it was today. The floors in the sitting room and dining room didn't have a fleck of dust on them and if you had never been in that house before you might believe that the furniture had never been used," Alex said as he rubbed his chin.

"The hair and blood on the beam too, Lady Sarah isn't tall enough to hit her head on any of the beams in that house, and her hair is a different length and colour to the bits that were matted in it," Arwyn replied.

"Did any of your colleagues search her belongings or ask any of the staff if they had seen any bloodstained clothes?" Mr Hunter looked at the constable with expectant eyes.

"No, and I can't imagine that Lady Sarah walking back to Grangeback in bloodstained clothes would have been missed by anyone in the village," Constable Evans said thoughtfully. Anything else that the two men might have said was interrupted by a loud rapping on the door of the police house.

Mr Hunter took charge of the kettle whilst the constable went to answer the door.

"Good day to you, constable, when you and Mr Hunter have finished your deliberations, I would be grateful if you would join me for dinner," Doctor Jack Hales said formally with a grave expression on his face.

"We'll come now, doctor," Alex announced as he made his way through the police house to stand beside the constable.

When he had heard the doctor's voice, he had taken the kettle off the fire and come to see what the physician wanted.

Doctor Hales looked at Alex and merely nodded in reply. Moments later, the three men were walking along the road to the doctor's home.

The doctor showed the two men into his drawing room where another man was waiting.

"I think you have both met Doctor Beardsley, the coroner. It seems you both might have some questions to ask him," Doctor Hales said as he poured each of them a drink.

Chapter 10

New Bailey Prison was a depressing construct that stood next to the newly built Salford Railway station. The station was due to be opened in a few weeks' time, but it acted as a useful landmark for those who were visiting the prison for the first time.

The prison entrance was on Stanley Street, and it was here that Mr Alexander Hunter found himself, between the two towers where men armed with muskets watched the approach to the prison from.

He felt cold bile rising in his throat as he thought about Lady Sarah being held within these walls, especially after everything he had seen, everything that Constable Evans had shown him and what the coroner had to say. It seemed the only reason the police believed Sarah was responsible was that she had seen all four of the victims just before they died.

Mr Harrison, Lady Sarah's solicitor, had arranged for

Mr Hunter to visit with her in prison and was stood by the gate talking to the warder guarding it. When the pair were finally granted entrance to the forbidding monolith to public order, they were escorted by two tall warders to the women's section of the prison and conducted to a small, dark room with only two chairs, a table and a tiny high window in it.

Alex sat at the table whilst Mr Harrison and the warders remained outside. Lady Sarah was brought in wearing a rough, grey dress with her hands chained together. Her face was drawn, and her skin had a nasty pallor. Her hands were cut and her arms badly bruised. Yet she maintained her composure and walked with the same grace and purpose that she had always shown since Alex had first met her.

It took all the self-control that Mr Hunter possessed not to throw the warder that brought her in against the wall and demand an explanation for her condition. Instead, he sat at the table and clasped his hands together so tightly, his fingers turned a deep red.

The warder unlocked the chains around the lady's wrists and left the pair in the room, ensuring that he locked the door behind him.

Sarah looked at Alex with a steady expression that in any other situation, would be read as annoyance.

"I'm sorry," Mr Hunter said as he stood up from the table and moved round to her ladyship's side. Sarah took a deep breath and closed her eyes. She sat perfectly still as Alex crouched down beside her and wrapped his arms about her.

She didn't cry as he held her, but buried her head in his shoulder and gripped his arm tightly with both of hers. Nothing was said by the pair for some minutes as they huddled together, but the young lady was the one to break the silence,

"You couldn't have known this was going to happen," Sarah soothed. The relief she felt at having him there left her feeling exhausted. She had pushed down all of her emotions since the moment that she knew that she was going to be arrested and hidden behind the mask that she had been taught to use by her mother.

Though she had been raised in the wilds of India, her mother had made sure to arm her daughter with the most important weapon of high society - the ability to seemingly rise above it all, to contain all emotion and present nothing but an air of serenity and disinterest to all those around them.

It was a mask that was serving her well inside the walls of the prison, but with Alex beside her, she felt her resolve beginning to crumble.

"If I hadn't gone, you wouldn't have been alone. I should have gone with you," Mr Hunter whispered his regrets into her hair.

"If you had, then you would have been arrested as well. I know that you love me, but you wouldn't be able to help me if you were locked up with me," Sarah replied gently.

“What do you want me to do?” Alex asked, feeling his own emotions threatening to overwhelm him.

"I want you to find whoever is responsible for this. Old Woakes was a kind man who didn't deserve to die in the way they said he did," Sarah sighed and pulled on Mr Hunter’s arm to bring him down to look her in the eyes.

“What about Nash, Allen and Thom?” Alex asked as he crouched beside Sarah and reached up to stroke the side of her face.

“Mr Thom was making some suits for me; I wanted them to be a surprise for you," Sarah smiled sadly and bit her lip to keep herself from crying.

“You went to have suits made for me?” Alex laughed slightly in spite of himself.

"When George comes back, you'll be the recognised son of a gentleman. You'll need some suits," Sarah told him.

“What about Allen then?” Mr Hunter asked. He knew that he didn’t have much time and though he wanted to argue with her ladyship over the importance of suits in his wardrobe, he needed as much information from Sarah as he could gather.

"Allen was asking me if there was any work he could give me, I sent him to several houses in the city that might be in need of someone to repair their pans," Sarah said. Mr Hunter thought about asking for the houses, but he doubted that the people who lived in the homes that Sarah would have sent the tinker to would have the time, energy or knowledge to perform such complicated murders.

"And Nash, did you ever meet him?" Alex asked as Sarah folded her hands in her lap, and he placed his free hand on hers.

"He wanted me to help him set up a new charitable foundation to help the children in the poor houses in the county. He was trying to speak to a number of people about it within the gentry. He thought titles would lend it more credence," Sarah explained. Alex nodded and took a deep breath. He could hear the warder beginning to jingle his keys outside of the door and knew that he would have to go much sooner than he had anticipated.

He leaned in suddenly and briefly kissed the lady. He felt tears falling onto his cheeks as Sarah began to silently cry.

Her hands reached into his hair and desperately held him for a few moments. When their lips parted, Mr Hunter whispered,

"I will find out who is responsible; I will get you out of here," he promised and stood up quickly, stepping back to a respectable distance before the door to the room was opened, and the warder walked in.

As Lady Sarah's chains were replaced, she kept her eyes locked with Alex's until the warder made her get to her feet and turn away from the hunter.

As she turned her back, she took a deep breath and

closed her eyes. It took a few seconds for her to regain her composure, but by the time she opened her eyes again, her mask was back in place.

The only sign that she had been crying were the drying tear tracks that ran down her cheeks. Mr Hunter turned away to face the wall instead of watching her disappear back into the prison.

“Did you get what you needed?” Mr Harrison asked as he stood in the doorway to the room.

"Yes," Alex replied bluntly.

"Then we should go," Mr Harrison instructed.

Chapter 11

When Mr Hunter returned to Stickleback that evening, Edryd and Derwyn were waiting with Doctor Hales to dine with him. The dinner was a silent, and stilted affair shrouded in the foul mood that seeing Sarah in prison had sunk Alex into.

The moment that he was finished eating, he rose from the table and went to lock himself in his father's study.

Nothing about the situation made any sense to him. There was no one that wanted to see Lady Sarah dead, not even Lady de Mandeville, and yet someone had made it his business to frame her for murder.

He spent the whole night sat in the brigadier's study, his mind picking over everything that Arwyn had told him, everything the coroner had told him and everything that Lady Sarah had said.

He had spent so long lost in his thoughts that he didn't realise that the night had ended. He didn't hear Mrs

Bosworth knock at the study door and he didn't hear her unlock the door from the outside.

"Mr Hunter, Constable Evans and Miss Wessex are here. You best come," Mrs Bosworth gently told him as she roused him from his musings and Pattison padded into the room and placed his head in Alex's lap.

Alex sighed, roughly stroked his Japanese hunting dog, and then stood to follow Mrs Bosworth to the drawing room where Miss Wessex and Arwyn were waiting.

The rest of the household had yet to rise, save for the servants, so it was an odd hour for anyone to be calling, yet the time of day didn't enter into Mr Hunter's thinking until he saw the bloodshot eyes of Elizabeth Wessex that told of desperate weeping.

"What's happened?" Alex frowned as he looked between the pair.

"Lord Cooper is missing," Arwyn said quietly.

"Mrs Bosworth, please take care of Miss Wessex. The constable and I are going to find our wayward neighbour," Alex sighed.

Miss Wessex made to open her mouth to thank the hunter, but instead of thanks, another flood of tears burst forth.

Alex saddled Black Guy and Harald for Arwyn and him to ride, and the pair set off for Duffleton Hall with Pattison trotting along beside them.

The Akita had spent far too long cooped up inside the house, and now that he was out, he raced off in all directions before he came back to try and tangle himself in the legs of Harald.

Both the constable and hunter were relieved when they reached Duffleton Hall and could leave the dog outside to race around the grounds.

The butler at Duffleton informed the two men that Lord Daniel Cooper hadn't been seen at the house for several days, but that he had been going to see his mother at Tatton Park.

The road between Stickleback Hollow and Tatton Park was a good road, though it was still the afternoon by the time Arwyn and Alex arrived at the great house belonging to the Egerton family.

Mrs Ruth Cooper was hardly pleased to see the two men and sent them away saying,

"I haven't seen my son since he took up with the

Wessex harlot."

There was nothing else that she would say to the men. By the time the constable and the hunter returned to Stickleback Hollow, the afternoon was fading fast, and neither man had eaten all day. They stopped at Wilson's Inn to eat.

"Do you think that Lord Cooper being missing is down to the Nursery Killer?" Arwyn asked in a low voice. Though they were surrounded by people that didn't believe that Lady Sarah could possibly have committed the murders, there were a lot of strangers in the village that seemed to be listening to every conversation with earnest interest.

"I don't know. You should go back to Duffleton and find out the date that Daniel left for Tatton Park. If he is dead and the Nursery Killer is responsible, then it will be enough to free Sarah - as long as she was already in prison when he vanished," Alex hissed as he let his eyes scan over the people sat in the inn to ensure that no one was listening to them.

"What are you going to do?" Arwyn asked as he drained the last of the ale from the mug in front of him.

"I am going to take Pattinson to search the woods. Daniel was going to Tatton Park, so I will search off the road and see if I can find any signs of where he might have gone," Alex replied.

"I will meet you at the police house later tonight, and I will tell you what I've found," Arwyn said as he stood up to leave.

"Are you going to spend any time talking to your brother and father at all?" Alex asked with an amused expression as Constable Evans made to turn away from him.

"You're a fine one to talk about estranged fathers," Arwyn said as he shot the hunter a dirty look over his shoulder.

"I made my peace with my father, yours came all this way, and he's still here. I don't think he's come just to see Doctor Hales or to keep Lady Sarah company," Alex shrugged in reply.

"Shouldn't you be doing something else?" Arwyn sighed.

"Think about it, my friend," Mr Hunter laughed as he watched Arwyn walk out of the inn, shaking his head.

Alex waited in Wilson's Inn for half an hour before

he left. He made sure that he had taken a mental note of all those in the inn that seemed to be paying too much attention to the drinks in front of them.

In his experience, those that focused their eyes on their drinks in a bar, especially when in a group, were those who were going to cause the most trouble. Their eyes were trained on a single spot so that their ears could focus on something else.

Pattinson had been sleeping whilst the two men ate, but now that Mr Hunter was on his feet again, the dog was only too happy to follow him.

Alex left Harald and Black Guy at the inn and made his way through the village and forests on foot. When he was done with his search and had spoken to Arwyn, he would lead the two horses back to Grangeback. But until then, the creatures had done enough for one day.

He made his way up through the trees, making sure that he doubled back to confuse anyone that might be following them.

Pattinson had his nose in the air and was on alert as everything in the way that Mr Hunter moved told the dog that they were hunting something.

When Alex was certain that they weren't being followed, he made his way to the road that led through the woods from Duffleton Hall.

The trees were the best place for the hunter to start his search as between the woods and Duffleton Hall there was nothing but open land and farms that would have seen anyone that attacked the young lord on the road.

In the woods, there were places for bandits, highwaymen and vagrants to hide, and though Alex did his best to ensure that the forests were free from danger, he had been away, and a wanderer on the road was as much of a threat to an unsuspecting rider as a gang that used the trees as their hunting grounds.

The light was bleeding from the sky as the hunter and the hunting dog reached the base of the Edge that rose out of the trees and cast a shadow across the village.

The Edge was a strange place that many people believe held strong magic, but to Alex, it was merely the site where he had saved Lady Sarah from three women and gained a hunting dog in the process.

The hunter had seen several signs that people had passed through the woods, but the trail he now followed was one that left him with an unsettled feeling in his stomach. When Pattinson suddenly shot off through the trees, Alex knew what he was going to find.

He followed after the dog, until he found the body of Lord Daniel Cooper, lying dead at the base of a tree. He had been staked to the ground, and the blood that was seeping through the coat that lay over his chest told Mr Hunter that the young lord had been cut open.

"Stay!" Mr Hunter ordered Pattinson to guard the body whilst he went to fetch Arwyn, hoping that Lord Daniel Cooper was the Rich man and that Lady Sarah would soon be free.

Chapter 12

NURSERY KILLER STILL AT LARGE

Today Lady Sarah Montgomery Baird Watson-Wentworth was released from prison after the discovery of the body of Lord Daniel Cooper. The young lord of Duffleton Hall disappeared on the road to Tatton Park the day after the lady was incarcerated. His body was discovered on the Edge last night, and the latest letter for the Nursery Killer was received this morning.

Tinker, Tailor, Soldier, Sailor, Rich man, Poor man, Beggar man, Thief, another body at your feet. Tinker slain, tailor too, next it was soldier and sailor, but I'm not through. Rich man's wealth couldn't save him from his end; when the reaper comes calling, riches have no aid to lend.

The police have no new leads in the case.

When Lady Sarah arrived home at Grangeback, her welcome home was almost the mirror image of her departure. Mr Hunter went to the prison to collect her with the carriage, and Sarah was so exhausted after her ordeal in prison, she fell asleep in Alex's arms on the journey home.

Doctor Hales, Constable Evans, Bosworth and Mrs Bosworth were all waiting on the manor house's steps when the carriage pulled up. Mr Hunter let Doctor Hales lead the lady into the house, where she was greeted by the household staff and Pattinson, all smiles and cheers.

Cooky was weeping with relief to see her mistress returned home, and both Derwyn and Edryd were happy to see their hostess safely back.

Mr Hunter made his way quietly through the house to wait for Lady Sarah in her room, the welcome home that the young lady was receiving was necessary, but not something that Alex was comfortable being part of.

When Mrs Bosworth eventually brought Lady Sarah to bed, she wasn't surprised to see Mr Hunter in the room, though it was clear from her expression that she didn't approve of a young man waiting in a young woman's room before they were married.

She didn't say a word to either of the pair and had to suppress a slight smile as Lady Sarah fell into Mr Hunter's arms.

Alex lay with his arms wrapped around Sarah that night. She woke up several times, shaking with fear, but his reassuring presence was enough to calm her and let her drift off back to sleep.

He hadn't expected to get much sleep that night and knew that it would be some time before she would be able to sleep soundly again.

After breakfast, Constable Evans arrived at the house to help Mr Hunter explain everything that they knew so far about the murders. When they had finished, Sarah sat and thought for a while before she spoke.

"So every victim so far can be connected to me. I turned down a marriage proposal from Daniel; the others all approached me or knew me in some way. Whoever this Nursery Killer is, he wanted people to believe I was responsible," Sarah blinked in disbelief.

"No, to begin with, that is what we all thought, but killing Daniel after it was reported in the newspaper that you had been arrested means that he didn't want that. He wanted people to know that you weren't the one murdering people, but I think he wants to hurt you with the murders,"

Alex explained gently.

"I agree with Hunter, though who the next victim will be I have no idea. Poor man leaves far too many people that it could be," Arwyn sighed.

"Then we need to find somebody who saw me, and the victims, and might have seen someone else. The village will be the best place to start, strangers stick out here much more than they do in Chester," Sarah said as she looked between the two men.

"We will go and see if we can find anyone that saw someone out of place around the village, but you need to rest," Mr Hunter said firmly as he sat down beside Sarah on the small settee.

"Hunter is right, you've been through enough without carting yourself around the village on a miserable day like this," the voice of Edward Egerton joined the conversation.

“Edward!” Sarah said with delight as she looked towards the door to the drawing room.

"Good morning, one and all. With the homecoming of one of my favourite neighbours, I felt that I should come and visit," Edward grinned as he shook droplets of rain from his top hat.

"Or escape from Mrs Cooper," Alex said dryly.

"That too, her grief has manifested in a rather peculiar manner, and the house of Egerton is one that the gentleman are currently fleeing because of it," Edward admitted as he sat in one of the high-backed chairs.

"Oh?" Sarah asked politely.

"Well, as you know, I am not one to gossip, but as the servants have already started to spread the news across the county, I might as well tell you. Lord Cooper left his fortune, and Duffleton Hall to Miss Wessex and Mrs Cooper is less than impressed about the whole situation. She has spent the whole morning screaming that Miss Wessex murdered her son, piggybacking on the murders that Lady Sarah committed," Edward smirked as he lounged in the armchair.

"Mrs Cooper believes that the well-bred ladies of England have all become killers with an unquenchable bloodlust?" Mr Hunter asked with a grin to match Edward's.

"Indeed, though unfortunately there is a Chief Constable hopefully who is willing to do whatever Mrs Cooper wishes as long as she supports his bid to take over from Captain Jonnes Smith," Edward replied sagely.

“Then it is even more important that you stay here, my lady. I am sure that Mr Egerton will be happy to keep you company along with your house guests whilst Mr Hunter and I go to the village," Constable Evans said from by the windows. Though he was comfortable enough around Alex and Sarah, he knew that the other members of the gentry were not as liberal as he friends and expected him to know his place.

"The constable is right, and I am sure that Doctor Hales will be coming to visit you to check on your health," Edward grinned, though he was trying to sound as carefree as he normally was, he couldn't hide the relief that he wouldn't have to return to Tatton Park for the rest of the day.

"We'll be back soon," Alex whispered to Sarah and gently squeezed her hand before he and Arwyn left the room to make their way down into the village. When the pair had gone, Edward fixed Sarah with a knowing look.

"I see that you are jumping from one scandal to the next," he chuckled.

“Excuse me?” Sarah frowned at her friend.

"Arrested for murder, now carrying on with Hunter?

You will be the sole topic of conversation in the court of St. James for years to come," Edward cried.

"I don't know what you are talking about," Sarah said innocently.

"I'm sure that you don't. Don't worry; I won't be the one to confirm the suspicious of thousands. I would advise a little more caution in future though," Edward winked.

Chapter 13

The day passed slowly for Lady Sarah, she was frustrated at being confined to the house, and the niceties that Edryd and Edward were trading in a gentlemanly battle of wits had fast drained her patience.

Derwyn and Doctor Hales were playing chess in the corner of the room, whilst Sarah sat and tried to read. After reading the same line for the tenth time without taking it in, she put down the book and left the library to take a turn in the garden.

Pattinson had stayed at the house with Lady Sarah whilst Alex went to the village with Arwyn, and he happily trotted at her ladyship's side as she walked around the small rose garden that lay to the side of the house.

It was a private enough place and afforded Sarah the illusion that she wasn't being held prisoner within the walls of the manor house. She knew that by keeping her at the house, her friends were making sure that she couldn't be connected to any further murders. But after her stint in prison, the last thing she wanted to hear was that there were places she could or couldn't go.

The fresh air was a blessing to her state of mind as she walked slowly between the different roses that the head gardener, Forbes, spent so long fussing over.

When Sarah had arrived at the house the year before, Forbes had planted a new variety of rose in the garden, the Meimafris. It stood beside the Kirlis, the Tucklucy and the Taytrust roses that were planted for the women in the brigadier's family and shared their names.

The light fragrance in the air was oddly comforting and let the stresses of the past few weeks melt from her shoulders. She was still worried about the whereabouts of Grace and Millie, but there was little she could do for the pair at present.

Instead, she focused her mind on the nursery rhyme and tried to think of who the next victims could be.

"Tinker, tailor, soldier, sailor, rich man, poor man, beggar man, thief," she recited aloud, and Pattinson cocked his head at the sound of her voice, "the first five victims have all been connected to me in some way, so the next three victims should be as well. Who do I know that is a poor man?" she asked Pattinson and sat down on the cast iron bench under the arbour to think.

The sky remained overcast, but the rains had stopped shortly before lunch. The scent of fresh earth and renewal that followed the rain was as the freedom that Sarah felt being out of the house.

"Henry Cartwright is the most obvious poor man, but he went with the brigadier," Sarah huffed and leant her chin on her fist as she thought.

"I'm sorry, your ladyship, but are you well? Only you seem to be talking to yourself," Forbes asked as he pottered around the rose garden.

"I am quite well, Forbes, merely thinking out loud. I apologise if I disturbed you," the young lady said as she sat up and smiled warmly at the gardener.

"No apology necessary, my lady. Though there is good news from Chester, I hear," Forbes replied as he inspected one of the rose bushes.

“Good news?” Sarah frowned.

"Yes, my lady, the Mitre Inn has been sold. Taken over by William Hughes, he's promised to transform it into a more genteel establishment," Forbes replied absently as he spotted some greenfly on the leaf of one of his beloved Rosa.

"What happened to William Lloyd?" Sarah asked with a nagging fear tugging at her sleeve.

"Some folk say he was robbed, others say he lost it all gambling on dice games, whatever the reason, he ran out of money and had to sell the inn to pay his debts," Forbes shrugged in reply.

"Forbes, I need you to find Stanley and Lee Baker, send them to Stickleback to find Constable Evans, tell him to go to Chester directly and find William Lloyd," Sarah said as she got to her feet and began to hurry back inside.

"As you say, my lady," Forbes said with a furrowed brow. He wasn't sure what had upset the young lady so much, but he was as certain now as he had ever been that the worries and problems of those above him were no of his concern.

When Stanley and Lee Baker found Constable Evans, he went to Chester immediately, whilst Mr Hunter returned to Grangeback with the two boys.

"You think William Lloyd will be the next victim?" Alex asked as Sarah met him in the hallway.

"Forbes told me that he lost everything, he's now a poor man, one that is connected to me and someone that we wouldn't think of as poor unless we knew about his troubles," Sarah replied.

"With any luck, you will be right, and Arwyn will arrive in time to stop him from being killed," Mr Hunter replied as the gong for dinner was sounded.

Sarah was silent through dinner and only picked at her food. The men talked jovially about fishing and hunting, which required no discourse from her ladyship.

After dinner, the doctor, Edward, Derwyn and Edryd sat down to play bridge, whilst Alex kept watch out of the windows for Arwyn's return.

Stanley and Lee Baker sat at Lady Sarah's feet and implored her to teach them how to play backgammon until she could no longer refuse.

By the time the police wagon rolled to a stop at the front of the manor, the Baker boys had fallen asleep by the fire, and the bridge game had long since ended.

Arwyn looked exhausted as he and Constable McIntyre entered the house, accompanied by Bosworth.

"What happened?" Alex was the first to speak.

"You were right, my lady, William Lloyd was the poor man," Constable Evans sighed.

"But you were too late," Sarah finished for him.

"Yes, my lady. The coroner says that he's been dead for several hours and the newspaper received another note from the killer. It will be in tomorrow's morning edition, but they let us see it first," Constable McIntyre said as he offered a scrap of paper to Lady Sarah.

She tentatively took the piece of paper and read through the rhyme scribbled upon it.

"Tinker, Tailor, Soldier, Sailor, Rich man, Poor man, Beggar man, Thief, another body at your feet. Poor man fell from his own high horse, he should've known that nothing in life stays the same course. Nearly all are gone, yet two remain. Can you stop me? Or will I win this game?" Sarah read out before she handed the piece of paper to Alex.

"What does this mean?" Mr Hunter asked crossly.

"I think you've been missing the obvious in all this," Derwyn's welsh lilt replied.

"The obvious?" Alex frowned.

"Whoever is killing these people connected to her ladyship wasn't trying to have her hanged for his crimes;

he's challenging her to stop him," Derwyn replied.

"My God, Edryd, your boy is a genius. It's so clear now. All the men knew Lady Sarah, they spoke to her, they have all had some form of contact with her. He's going after these people to get your attention. When you didn't make the connection, he sent you to prison to force your involvement," Doctor Hales exclaimed.

"What about Lloyd though, there's no way that he was connected to Lady Sarah," Edward scoffed.

"He has helped us in the past," Sarah said slowly.

"How many people knew about that?" Edryd asked.

"Almost none," Mr Hunter replied.

"So whoever this person is, they've been watching you for some time and to challenge you to catch them and to stop them from killing, they must know at least some of what has happened since you arrived in England," Constable Evans concluded.

"But how does that help us?" Sarah asked helplessly.

"We can't say yet, my lady, but some other constables are meeting us at the police house in the village tomorrow. We'll do all we can to help. In the meantime, it might be best if you got some rest," Constable McIntyre replied.

"A good idea, constable," Doctor Hales agreed.

"Bosworth, can you please ensure that rooms have been made up for Mr Egerton, the good doctor and the two constables, please? I think that it is best that no one travels home at this late hour," Lady Sarah said calmly before she bid everyone good night and left the room.

"She made a mistake there," Edward hissed into Alex's ear.

"And what's that?" Alex replied with a confused expression.

"She didn't ask for Bosworth to make you up a room," Edward winked. Mr Hunter scowled slightly and opened his mouth to say something, but Edward hushed him, "I'm not going to tell anyone, but for appearance's sake, make to leave and come back in through the French windows when everyone else has gone to bed," he urged his friend and left Alex wondering how many times Edward Egerton had used the same ploy to avoid scandals of his own.

Chapter 14

The gathering of the police constables at the police house in Stickleback Hollow was easy enough to arrange without causing any suspicion amongst the rest of the constabulary. The higher-ranking officers were still trying to curry favour with the powerful members of society in case Captain Jonnes Smith didn't return.

This meant that they were all blissfully unaware of the actions of most of their subordinates. Nobody missed Constable McIntyre that night, and nobody commented on how strange it was that Constables Meyers, Cantello, Clewes, Kelly and McGill all departed for Stickleback Hollow the following morning.

Constables Evans and McIntyre had to hook the horses back into their traces to drive the police wagon back to the police house, but they were still there before the other constables arrived.

Now that the evidence had cleared Lady Sarah and

there were no other suspects, the police were back to square one, but with Derwyn's insight and the investigation that Arwyn and Alex had conducted, they were in a better position than any of them could have hoped for.

No one that Mr Hunter and the constable had spoken to in the village had seen anything unusual on the day that Old Woakes had died, but the two men had not spent long talking to the villagers before the Baker boys had been sent to fetch them.

"Mrs Cooper has been putting pressure on the higher up to open an investigation into Miss Wessex as the murderer of her son," Constable Clewes said when the men had all assembled in the police house.

"Then we should at least see if there is anything to her allegations. Constable Meyers and I will go and talk to Mrs Cooper and Miss Wessex," Constable Kelly replied.

"Good, then the rest of us can go to the village and see if anyone saw any strangers in Stickleback Hollow, not just on the day that Archibald Woakes was murdered but the days before and after it as well," Constable McGill said firmly.

"How many days on either side of the murder?"

Constable Cantello asked.

"No more than three," Constable McGill replied.

"I'm going to stay here and see if I can work out who the beggar man might be. If we can't find anything out in the village or from Mrs Cooper, then we may be able to catch the Nursery Killer before he kills the beggar man," Arwyn said. The other constables left to go about their assigned tasks as Constable Evans sat down to think of the men that had been in contact with Lady Sarah and could be described as a beggar man.

Chapter 15

Mr Edward Egerton and Mr Hunter left Grangeback not long after the two constables had. The pair had decided that they need some fresh air and would go fishing for the day.

At least that had been what they told Mrs Bosworth. In actuality, Alex wanted to talk to Edward about Lady Sarah. Since the hunter had found himself in love with the young lady, he hadn't had anyone to confide in about it - or to ask advice from. So fishing in the lake all day was a comfortable way for the pair to talk without worrying that anyone would happen upon their conversation.

This, however, left Lady Sarah to her own devices. With the police no longer concerned that Sarah was the murderer, she was free to move about as she wished once more.

As she hadn't had a chance to pass on her condolences to Miss Wessex or any of the household at Duffleton Hall in the wake of Lord Daniel's death, Lady

Sarah decided to ride to the great house and faithfully promised Mrs Bosworth that she would be back in time for dinner.

The doctor had taken Derwyn and Edryd to Chester Racecourse for the day, which left the house free of visitors for the first time in weeks, though they would be back in time for dinner; Mrs Bosworth had an opportunity to put the house back to rights.

There was a feeling of hope in the air as Sarah set off with Black Guy. Rather than riding straight there, the young lady decided to first visit Wilson's Inn to see if the innkeeper had any news for her.

It was a warm and bright spring day, and Sarah was in no hurry to complete her journey. She enjoyed basking in the soft spring sunshine as she rode and was almost disappointed when she came to the courtyard at the inn. As she dismounted, none of the stable boys were in sight, and the only other person there was a man limping across the courtyard wearing a rough, thick cloak and a large-brimmed hat.

As the man hobbled past Sarah, a scrap of paper fell from his cloak and landed in the mud beside her.

"Excuse me!" Lady Sarah called out as she bent down to pick up the piece of paper, but by the time she looked up, the man had gone.

She rushed out of the courtyard to see if she could find the man on the street, but there was no sign of him there either.

Lady Sarah stood there for a few moments and puzzled over where the man had gone until Black Guy nudged her arm with his muzzle.

She laughed at the horse and was about to lead him back into the courtyard when she paused and unfolded the scrap of paper.

You'll find what you're looking for at the Pearson Farm.

Sarah felt that it was odd that this piece of paper should happen to fall at her feet from the hands of a mysterious cripple, but she knew that the Pearson Farm was not far from the village; that it wouldn't do any harm to see if the man was there and return the paper to him.

She mounted Black Guy and set off down the road

that led towards Duffleton Hall. Pearson Farm lay halfway between the village and the hall, and it had been abandoned for as long as Sarah had been in England.

The farmer who had run the farm had died, leaving behind a wife and three young children that had become so burdened by debt that the farm had been seized and the mother and children had been taken to the debtors' prison.

As she arrived at the farm, it was completely deserted, but the stable had fresh hay and water in one of the stalls. Lady Sarah led Black Guy into the stable, removed his bridle and saddle and left them slung over the stable door.

She hadn't seen any sign of living at the farm, other than the well-kept stable, but concluded that if someone were living there, they didn't want anyone to be able to tell from looking at the outside of the farm buildings.

When she was certain that Black Guy was settled and couldn't get out of the stable, she made her way to the main farmhouse and tried the door. It was locked.

The windows were all boarded up, except for one that had lost the board on the second floor. Ivy clung to trellis and made its way up to the window that wasn't boarded up.

With a great amount of effort, Sarah began to use the plant and trellis to scale the side of the farmhouse until she reached the window. It wasn't open, but it didn't take much for the young lady to open it with one hand and slip through it into the house.

The dust was thick on the floor as she clambered inside, and the upstairs showed no signs that anyone had been there or at least been sleeping upstairs. She made her way cautiously down the staircase, flinching at every creaking floorboard.

When she reached the ground floor, the dust patterns on the floor changed. There were footprints and drag marks through the dust that told of someone making frequent trips into one room of the house.

Sarah hadn't heard any sound aside from the creaking floorboards, her pounding heart and her footsteps echoing in the house that was empty of furniture, so she didn't expect to see anyone in the room as she pushed the door open.

There was no one there, but the room was by no means empty. Sarah had never seen anything like it before in her life. In the centre of the room was a desk with scraps of paper piled up on one side of it and a quill and inkpot lay on the other side of it.

The ink was cheap, the paper coarse and the quill looked like it had been fashioned out of a crow's feather. On the walls, the newspaper reports about the Nursery Killer had all been nailed up, and certain parts of the stories had been circled with what looked like coal dust. Next to each newspaper report was the name of each victim scrawled on a scrap of paper with their part in the nursery rhyme beside it. Underneath this scrap of paper was nailed another that seemed to list a crime that each victim had never been punished for.

The hairs on the back of Sarah's neck were all stood on end as she looked over the walls and came to four scraps of paper that didn't have newspaper articles nailed beside them.

Mr Andrew Christopher the verger – Beggar man
Mr A. Hunter the groundskeeper- Thief

Tears welled up in Sarah's eyes as she realised the danger that Alex was in. She turned to flee from the room and make her way back through the window that she had climbed through but found her way barred by the man dressed in the rough, thick cloak.

He had moved silently; Sarah didn't know how long he had been stood there or even if he had been following her since she entered the house.

"So curious, so clever," a wheezing voice came from underneath the large brimmed hat that made Sarah begin to tremble where she stood.

"You left me that note," she choked in reply.

"I needed you to see all of this. You understand not having justice. Your parents died, and no one paid for their murder. This was the only way to show the world these terrible men," the voice rasped, and the man took a step towards Sarah, causing the lady to retreat into the room.

"They're not terrible men, none of them were," Sarah cried.

"Oh, they were all guilty men," the voice spat back nastily.

"Alex isn't. He isn't a thief, he never stole anything," Sarah looked around desperately for another way out of the room, but there was none to be found.

"He's a nasty little thief, and his death will be fitting for his crime," the voice crowed.

"What do you think he stole?" Sarah asked, hoping she could reason with the voice.

"Your virtue," the voice hissed, and the man moved. He moved so quickly that Sarah didn't know what was happening. The first she knew was that the man was behind her, gripping her arm, forcing it up her back and pushing her over the table.

He grabbed hold of her other arm and manhandled it around her back as Sarah struggled to free herself from his vice-like grip. She felt him tying her wrists together and then her ankles.

He lowered her gently to the floor and left her lying so that she could stare up at the last two names.

"You'll be safe here until my work is done. Then I will let you go. I thought you would be the one person that could understand why I am doing this, but maybe you're not as clever as I thought," the voice wheezed before the man silently left the room.

Chapter 16

Grangeback was oddly still when Edward and Alex returned to the great house. They had spent hours relaxing by the lake and though it had taken Mr Hunter a while to feel comfortable enough to ask Mr Egerton's advice about the lady.

There wasn't much that Edward could tell Alex about Lady Sarah as a person, but he was able to provide insight into the female mind that Mr Hunter had never been privy to.

It was also a chance for them both to forget the burdens of the Nursery Killer. Edward could forget about Mrs Cooper's accusations and the atmosphere it had created at Tatton Park too, and enjoy the company of his school friend.

They had managed to catch enough fish to fill the wicker basket that Cooky had given them, even with Pattinson charging into the water every few minutes at the start of the day.

The dog had soon become bored with racing into the lake and had been content to lie by the shore and sleep in the spring sunshine.

The two men and the dog arrived back at the house moments before Doctor Hales, Edryd and Derwyn returned from their day at the races.

"I see you had a successful day," the doctor said in greeting as he climbed out of the carriage and the five men went into the house together.

Cooky was happy with the fish that had been brought and rushed off to the kitchen to prepare them for dinner.

“Where is Lady Sarah?” the doctor asked Bosworth as the butler prepared drinks for the five men in the library.

"Her ladyship hasn't returned from Duffleton Hall yet. She did say she would be back in time for dinner," Bosworth replied.

The men thought no more about her absence until the gong for dinner was sounded. They hadn’t expected to see her return, but when they reached the dining room, she wasn’t there.

"Mrs Bosworth, can you send the Baker boys to find Constable Evans," Alex asked the housekeeper quietly. Mrs Bosworth nodded and went to send the two boys on their way.

Dinner was served and cleared away, and there was still no sign of Lady Sarah. When Arwyn arrived at the house, he was at a loss to explain her absence too. No one had seen her in the village since earlier that day when she had been seen on the road to Duffleton Hall.

"Maybe she decided to spend the night there," Edward offered, though he didn't believe his own suggestion was correct.

"If she were spending the night at Duffleton Hall, she would have sent word that she wasn't coming back. After everything that's happened with the murders, she wouldn't leave us wondering where she was," Mr Hunter replied, shaking his head.

"Then we need to organise a search party to find her," Edryd said, clapping his hands together. Doctor Hales smiled in spite of himself as he thought of all the search parties that had been formed since Lady Sarah's arrival in the village.

Prior to the young lady's arrival, the only search party that had been organised was the one to search for Arwyn when he had run away from home. Now it seemed to Doctor Hales that search parties were being organised every few months to search for one person or another.

"I'm afraid that searching for her ladyship will have to wait, sirs. Constable Kelly is here, Constable Evans, it seems that another body has been found," Bosworth said as he came into the library where the six men were waiting.

"Who is it?" Arwyn asked.

"The verger, Mr Christopher, constable," Bosworth replied.

"Is it the Nursery Killer?" Alex asked.

"Constable Kelly seems to think so, sir," Bosworth said.

"Doctor, will you wait here in case Lady Sarah comes home? Constable Evans has a body to deal with and Mr Egerton, and I will ride to Duffleton Hall to see if Lady Sarah is there. With the killer having struck tonight, the fewer people that are moving around in the dark, the better," Mr Hunter sighed.

"Of course, Derwyn and I can finish our chess

tournament whilst we wait for news, though Edryd might be a useful companion for your journey to Duffleton Hall. He knows a few of the staff there," the doctor suggested, and Alex nodded his agreement.

Constable Kelly was stood on the steps of Grangeback with the police wagon waiting behind him. The two men climbed up to drive the wagon and were on their way down to the village before the grooms had begun to saddle the horses for Mr Hunter's riding party.

When Arwyn and Constable Kelly arrived at the church, the Reverend Percy Butterfield was talking to Constable Meyers.

"The killer posted the note through the vicar's door," Constable Cantello said as Arwyn climbed down from the police wagon and was handed the note.

"He didn't send it to the newspaper?" Constable Evans asked as he unfolded the scrap of paper.

"No, we don't know why. Maybe he wanted us to find the verger now for some reason," Constable McGill shrugged as Arwyn began to read the note.

Tinker, Tailor, Soldier, Sailor, Rich man, Poor man,

Beggar man, Thief, another body at your feet. Beggar man now has left this mortal plane, all his begging, claiming innocence in vain. The thief is the last on my list now, the last act before my final bow.

"This doesn't seem like it is going to end well," Arwyn sighed as he folded up the note.

"Did the verger have any connection to Lady Sarah at all?" Constable McIntyre asked as he joined the group of policemen.

"I don't think her ladyship ever met him. There wasn't really anything he would need to talk to Lady Sarah about," Constable Evans replied.

"The reverend said that the verger had been visiting the wealthier homes in the area to ask for donations to the church," Constable McIntyre replied.

"So he may have been to ask Lady Sarah for money," Constable McGill sighed.

"Asking for money makes him a beggar in the eyes of the Nursery Killer?" Constable Cantello suggested.

"Perhaps, but Lady Sarah is missing. I am beginning to wonder whether this is not a challenge to her, but more than the murderer is trying to impress her," Arwyn sighed as he rubbed his temples with his fingertips.

"What do you mean, her ladyship is missing?" Constable McIntyre frowned.

"She didn't arrive back at Grangeback this evening. She went to Duffleton Hall this afternoon to pass on her condolences to Miss Wessex and promised Mrs Bosworth that she was going to be back in time for dinner," Constable Evans explained.

"Is she missing or did she just spend the night at Duffleton Hall?" Constable Kelly asked with a slight frown.

"Mr Hunter has gone with Mr Egerton and Mr Evans to find that out. They should be back in a few hours," Arwyn sighed.

Chapter 17

The room had long since fallen dark in the abandoned farmhouse. Lady Sarah had been straining at the ropes around her wrists and ankles for hours as she lay on the dusty floor. Panic had seized her, to begin with, but when the murderer had left her alive and left her alone in the farmhouse, she had been able to calm herself enough to know what she needed to do.

She had to free herself and reach Mr Hunter before the Nursery Killer did. She worked on freeing one of her wrists instead of trying to get them both out of the ropes.

It had still been light when she had started trying to work her wrist free, and it had been a good hour since it had fallen dark. Her wrist ached from the friction burn that the rope had caused, but she finally managed to get it free.

Her body ached from lying in the same position, and the pain was intense as she moved her shoulders and managed to lie on her back. She lay still for a few minutes before she sat up and untied the bonds about her feet.

As she picked herself up off the floor, Sarah knew that she was in no condition to ride back to Grangeback. She could barely walk, but she managed to stagger to the door of the farmhouse.

It had been locked from the inside when she arrived and had to climb through the window, but now she was in the farmhouse, she could open the door, and she stumbled through it towards the stable.

Black Guy was still in the stable, but it was so dark that it was hard for the lady to make out where the horse was and almost impossible for her to saddle the horse again without a lantern.

Sarah opened the stable door, picked up the saddle and bridle and threw them onto the horse's back. She draped one arm over the Black Guy's neck and gripped his mane with the other.

Lady Sarah leant against the horse as the two of them began to move out of the stable yard and towards the road.

Chapter 18

There was no sign of Lady Sarah on the road, and no one at Duffleton Hall had seen her either. Alex had wanted to search the woods for her, but Edryd and Edward had both persuaded him that any search would be best left until morning.

The three men and Pattinson had turned back to Grangeback, though Mr Hunter had decided that it was best if he spent the night at the lodge instead of the main house.

He wished Edryd and Edward a goodnight after they had stabled their horses and then made his way on foot across the grounds to his home.

The night was cool and clear, and Pattinson walked at Mr Hunter's heels as the pair cast long, faint shadows on the lawns.

When they reached the trees around the lodge, Alex could hear the soft and slow pad of hooves across the forest. He paused to look around but couldn't see the animal that was moving around.

He smiled to himself as he realised that it must be a deer as no horse with a rider could move that softly or that slowly.

Pattinson curled up by the fire in the lodge after he charged through the lodge's back door ahead of Alex. The hunter smiled at the dog's keenness to sleep after traipsing around the Cheshire countryside.

Mr Hunter wearily clambered up the stairs, he was worried about where Sarah was, but he was also aware that if he was too tired, he wouldn't be able to do much to find her. He had resolved to sleep until first light and then set out to search for her.

He lay down on his bed and pulled the blankets over him. It felt like his head had barely touched the pillow when he was woken by Pattinson growling downstairs. Alex sat bolt upright and swung his feet over the edge of the bed. His feet touched the floor as Pattinson's growling turned to yelping.

Mr Hunter rushed out of his room and reached the top of the stairs. At the foot of the stairs, looking up at Alex was a man in a rough cloak and a large-brimmed hat.

In the man's hand was a gun that was aiming at Mr Hunter's chest.

"It may be fairly gauche, but I am running out of time to finish my work, and the one person I thought would understand what I was doing was, quite frankly, a disappointment," the man said with resignation in his voice.

"Why are you doing this?" Alex asked as he carefully watched the gun instead of the man.

"It would take too long to explain, and I doubt that you have the capacity to understand my motivations. But you do not need to understand them. Tinker, tailor, soldier, sailor, rich man, poor man, beggar man and now thief. Another body at your feet. Escaped their crimes through trick or lie, left me no choice, tinker, tailor, soldier, die. Not my best work, but a fitting way to end this merry dance, don't you think?" the man said, and Alex heard a gun cock before it fired.

He expected to feel some form of shock or pain as the bullet struck his body, but nothing came. Instead, the man fell forward onto the bottom of the stairs and revealed Lady Sarah stood behind him.

In her hand was her pistol and she was shaking

badly. Mr Hunter rushed down the stairs and stepped over the Nursery Killer's body to take Sarah into his arms. He held her for a moment.

"No, Pattinson needs you more," Sarah said as she stared at the body of the murderer on the floor. Mr Hunter went over to his dog and found that he had been stabbed twice and was in very bad condition.

"I need to take him to the main house; Doctor Hales should still be there," Alex said as he looked at Pattinson's wounds.

"Black Guy is outside, take him. Tell them what happened. I'll wait here," Sarah's voice trembled as she spoke, but Alex had little choice but to do what Sarah said.

Chapter 19

The sound of Mr Hunter pounding on the door brought Bosworth to the door with two footmen flanking him on either side.

When they found Alex on the doorstep with Pattinson in his arms, Bosworth threw open the door and sent the footmen to raise the rest of the household.

Doctor Hales was the first out of bed followed by Mrs Bosworth. The housekeeper cleared the chairs away from the table in the dining room and put a white cloth down for the doctor to work on Pattinson.

Edryd took Mr Hunter into the library to sit down with a drink whilst the doctor worked with Mrs Bosworth's help. Derwyn and Edward were the last to come down the stairs with the Baker boys.

When Alex began to explain what had happened at the lodge, Edward sent Stanley and Lee to fetch the constables from the village. Edward then went to dress so that he could go back to the lodge with Mr Hunter to fetch Lady Sarah.

Derwyn decided to go with the two gentlemen to wait for his brother and the other constables to arrive at the lodge.

Edryd stayed to keep Cooky and the rest of the staff out of the doctor's way whilst he worked on saving Pattinson's life.

When Mr Hunter, Mr Egerton and Mr Evans reached the lodge, Sarah was sat in the armchair opposite the fire.

She was sat in the dark staring at the empty grate. Her hands were folded in her lap, and she was trembling as she tried to control her breathing.

Alex went over to her side and knelt down, gently resting his hand on hers; placing the lantern he carried on the floor in front of them both.

Edward and Derwyn made their way over to look at the body that was lying on the stairs, where he had fallen when Sarah shot him.

Blood had stained the wood of the stairs around the body, but the two men were happy enough to leave him where he was until the police came.

"Where have you been?" Alex whispered to Sarah as he rubbed her hands with his.

"That man, he was at Wilson's Inn. He dropped a note that told me to go to a farm. He was the Nursery Killer. All the victims were on the wall in the farmhouse – the verger, is he dead?" Sarah asked as she looked over at the hunter.

"Yes, he was killed sometime this afternoon or evening," Alex replied softly.

"I came to warn you that you were next. He didn't search me when he found me in the farmhouse," Sarah explained.

"He found you? Did he hurt you?" Alex asked as he started to carefully look over the young lady for any sign of injury.

"No, he tied me up when I didn't approve of what he was doing. He told me everything. I couldn't let him kill you," Sarah said as her eyes filled with tears, and she slipped from the chair into Alex's arms.

The pair sat on the floor, Mr Hunter holding Lady Montgomery Baird Watson-Wentworth as she cried. The couple were still holding each other when the constables arrived.

After Mr Hunter had told Constables Evans and Kelly what had happened, Lady Sarah took the men to the abandoned farmhouse and showed them the lair of the Nursery Killer.

By the time Lady Sarah, Derwyn, Edward and Alex arrived back at Grangeback, the doctor had finished operating on Pattinson.

The dog was lying by the fire in the library on a collection of blankets and pillows that Mrs Bosworth and Cooky had arranged for him.

The two women were sat either side of the dog, fussing over him as he whined in pain.

"How is he, doctor?" Alex asked as Mrs Bosworth left Pattinson to come and take care of Lady Sarah.

"He will heal well; Cooky and Mrs Bosworth have elected to look after him whilst the worst of his injuries heal. He's a very lucky pup to have so many people to fuss over him," Doctor Hales smiled and shook Alex's hand.

Mrs Bosworth took Lady Sarah upstairs to rest whilst Alex sat with Pattinson.

"I think it would be best if you stayed here tonight,

Mr Hunter," Bosworth told the hunter as he offered him something to drink.

"The police will want the lodge to be left empty for a while, so it might be for the best," Alex smiled in reply.

Chapter 20

Miss Grace Read had never been so miserable in her life. She was cold, and her body ached from being tied up for so long. She had no idea where she was or where Miss Millie Roy was, but she knew that they hadn't left England yet.

"What are we supposed to do?" one of her captors asked the others as they were sat around a small fire.

They were sheltering in the mouth of an abandoned mine, and the fire was kept small so that the smoke didn't overwhelm the occupants in the mine.

Grace was being kept in a natural alcove in the mine wall, away from the entrance and away from the fire. She had no way of getting past the three men that were now huddled around the fire, even if she had a way of freeing herself.

She felt alone and scared for herself and worried about what had happened to Millie.

"I don't know. We were supposed to take the ship to

France and then make our way to Lichtenstein, but this blasted situation in China," another man replied.

"They can't stop ships sailing forever. We just have to wait until we get word from the captain that he can leave," the third man said.

"So we just have to wait here until then?" the first man asked.

"That's all we can do," the third man shrugged.

"What about the women? We have to keep them both?" the second man asked.

"We were given our orders. We follow them, or we'll be found floating in the river," the third man replied.

Chapter 21

Mr Hunter didn't sleep that night. He spent the small hours of the morning sat beside Pattinson in the library thinking about his father and everything that had happened since the brigadier had left so unexpectedly. He wondered what was happening in China and what was going to happen to Sarah over the Nursery Killer.

Alex knew that he wasn't going to be able to go back to the lodge for some time, but he was also not sure that he wanted to.

He had never wanted to have the privilege that George had tried to provide for him, but since Lady Sarah had arrived, he was willing to embrace all of it for her.

Mr Hunter knew that she would never ask him to, but it was for that reason that he was willing to do it. Mrs Bosworth was the first to find him the next morning, and the two discussed Alex moving into the main house on a permanent basis.

Edward, Edryd and Derwyn had all been invited to stay indefinitely by Lady Sarah, so Alex being added to the household wouldn't raise any eyebrows.

Doctor Hales had spent the night at Grangeback after operating on Pattinson and went to check on Lady Sarah's condition after all that she had been through.

When the doctor arrived at her room, he found the young lady was feeling weak and vomiting. She was leaning over the basin in her room, so the doctor helped her back to bed.

"Are you feeling quite well?" the doctor asked as he perched on the edge of her bed.

"I have been feeling tired and sick for some time. I thought it was the stress of the brigadier leaving, and Grace and Millie being kidnapped, but my back now hurts and my chest," Lady Sarah explained.

"Your chest or your breasts?" the doctor smiled.

"The latter," Sarah replied stiffly.

"I see, from what you have said, my lady, I believe you need to speak to Mr Hunter rather soon and write a letter to your guardian," Jack said as he patted her hand.

"And why is that? Is there something wrong?" Sarah

asked worriedly.

"Not at all, though it may be something of a scandal, it is nothing that is wrong as far as I can see," the doctor replied kindly.

"What is it then?" Sarah frowned.

"You, my dear lady, are pregnant," Doctor Hales grinned.

"Pregnant?" Sarah asked with wide eyes.

"Yes, and for what it is worth, I think the pair of you will not only be very happy together but will make excellent parents," the doctor said warmly.

"What if he doesn't want this?" Sarah asked worriedly.

"I can assure you, I have never seen Mr Hunter in love before, but he certainly is now. He will be overjoyed by the news. I also think that anyone who has the good judgement to keep Arwyn's father and brother here until he has the sense to repair his broken bridges will make the best sort of mother," Jack replied.

"What of the scandal?" Sarah asked.

"You have powerful friends who will protect you from most of it, and with George recognising Alex as his son;

your son will never be denied anything. I know that this is unexpected news, but it is a good thing," the doctor assured her.

"Then I should write to the brigadier? How do I know where to send the letter?" Sarah asked.

"To the British Consulate, they will find a way to get the letter to him," the doctor replied kindly.

"Do you think he will be back soon?" Sarah sighed as she laid back against her pillows and closed her eyes.

"I hope so. I am sure that things cannot be so bad overseas that he will have to be gone for so long, but I am certain that it is the fate of Grace and Millie that has you wanting him to return," the doctor said as he stood up and went to pour the young lady a glass of water from the pitcher that sat on her dressing table.

"They have been missing for too long, and no one is looking for them," Sarah said, shaking her head.

"I will talk to Constable Evans, if he and his brothers can put aside their differences for a while, they may be able to find them both. I will see if Constable Clewes can stay to take over Arwyn's duties," the doctor said as he placed the glass on Sarah's nightstand.

"Mr Hunter should go with them," Sarah said firmly as she opened her eyes and looked at the doctor.

"He should be here with you," the doctor smiled down at her.

"If he goes with the Evans brothers, then Grace and Millie will come home, and then I will tell him about the baby," Lady Sarah replied.

"If you think that is best, then I will talk to Mr Hunter, Constable and Derwyn Evans and Constable Clewes," the doctor agreed begrudgingly.

"Thank you, I will write to the brigadier, and hopefully we will all be home at Grangeback before this baby is born," Sarah sighed.

~*~*~

Love the book? Need to know what's next in Stickleback Hollow?

Far from home, on the business of the Empire, lives and silver are on the line. Short on allies, the Far East is filled with malevolent enemies and deadly mysteries.

Get ***What Became of Henry Cartwright?*** now!

~*~*~

Looking for more than just books? You can get the latest releases from me, signed paperbacks and hardbacks, mugs, t-shirts, journals and much more from my Read Round the Clock Shopify store.

~*~*~

Love the Mysteries of Stickleback Hollow? Not caught up with the rest of the series, then jump back to *A Thief in Stickleback Hollow,* Book 1 in the Mysteries of Stickleback Hollow and see how it all began.

~*~*~

Want to help a reader out? Review are crucial when it comes to helping readers choose their next book and you can help them by leaving just a few sentences about this book as a review. It doesn't have to be anything fancy, just what you liked about the book and who you think might like to read it.

If you don't have time to leave a review or don't feel confident writing one, recommending a book to your family, friends and co-workers can help them choose their next book, so feel free to spread the word.

Personal Note

Keith, whom this book is dedicated to, was a man I met only a year before his death. Yet, he had a profound influence on my life. He was a man of charity, warmth, wisdom and love. He could be irritable, but always offered intellectual debate and was never afraid to ask for advice from those who were better versed in a subject than he. I miss him dearly and hope that when my time comes that I will be as warmly remembered as he is.

Historical Note

The Directorate of Military Intelligence was the first incarnation of the British Intelligence service that was founded by Major Thomas Best Jervis in 1854 during the Crimean War. It was subsumed into the Ministry of Defence in 1964, and the Directorate of Military Intelligence was absorbed into the Defence Intelligence Staff.

The Defence Intelligence Staff was created by absorbing Military Intelligence, Air Intelligence and Naval Intelligence and is different from the UK's intelligence agencies MI5, MI6 and GCHQ.

In 1903 William Melville campaigned for the creation of the Secret Intelligence Service. It was known as the Secret Service Bureau and developed until it had 19 intelligence departments MI1 to MI19, though only MI5 and MI6 remain active to this day. William Melville began by hiring a

Courage Brewery representative in Hamburg to spy for him, and in 1909 Melville went to Germany to recruit more agents.

After World War I broke out, the Secret Service Bureau received more funding, and it was attached to the newly established G-section that was focused on investigating people that were suspected of being enemy agents. Melville also founded a spy school opposite the War Office at Whitehall Court. However, he died before the close of World War I in February 1918 from kidney failure. Melville was the first spymaster in the UK and thus is credited as the first holder of the positions of the Director-General of MI5 and Head of SIS, both from 1903 to 1909.

Intelligence officers and spies have served in the military during many conflicts, including the Napoleonic Wars.

Clothes horses are not replicas of actual horses. Wooden clothes horses were the norm in Victorian times. They were made from two iron frames that were placed a suitable distance apart and had wooden poles or laths (between four and six of them) that ran between them.

The frames were attached to a pulley system that meant the frames could be lowered from the ceiling, have wet clothes hung over the poles, and then hoisted up to the ceiling again so that clothes could dry without taking up space in the house.

They were also used in kitchens to hang utensils and some types of food from them such as herbs and game.
Clothes horses still exist now, but instead of an elaborate pulley system, they are metal frames that can be folded away when they are not in use. There are even some now that can be plugged in and the metal poles that washing is hung on heat up to aid in the drying process.

Stoves for cooking were first invented in 1800 when a man called Benjamin Thompson created the Rumford Stove. The idea was that it could be used to heat several pots rather than cook as we would now use an oven. However, the Rumford Stove was far too large to be put in people's homes. It wasn't until 1834 that a similar stove was patented in America. It was called the Oberlin Stove and worked on the same principle, only it was much smaller than the Rumford Stove. Over the course of 30 years, over 90,000 Oberlin Stoves were sold, and they were powered by either wood or coal depending on the household.

In 1851, the Great Exhibition saw the first gas stoves appear, but they were not widely used in domestic homes until the 1890s as people were afraid of them exploding and considered them a health risk.

It wasn't until 1893 that the first electric stove appeared and it wasn't until 1930 that electric stoves became advanced enough for people to use in their homes.

The Cheshire Police committee met on 3rd February 1857 after a committee met in 1856 to advise on how to apply the new County and Borough Police Act 1856. The Act meant that the Justices had to establish a paid police force for every county in Great Britain. The Cheshire Police committee met at the Crewe Arms Hotel with Mr Trafford Trafford as the chair. The Cheshire Constabulary was then officially formed on 20th April 1857 – a full 30 years after A Thief in Stickleback Hollow is set, but for the sake of artistic license I shifted the timescale.

However, Captain Thomas Jonnes Smith was the first Chief Constable, though I imagine that he was a completely different character to the one portrayed in these books and was not part of a secret spy agency that went into China to help bring an end to the Opium Wars.

In 1857 the Cheshire Constabulary had its headquarters at 4 Seller Street in Chester, but this has been moved several times. In 1862 it was moved to 1 Egerton Street, then to 113 Foregate Street in 1870. In 1883 it was moved to 142 Foregate, where it remained until 1967. In 1967 a new headquarters was opened on Nuns Road, Chester, that had been purpose-built over three years for the police. Then in 2003, the headquarters was moved to a new purpose-built home at Clemonds Hey, Winsford.

In 1934 the Criminal Investigations Department or CID was opened at the 142 Foregate headquarters and radios were also introduced to allow officers to communicate whilst on duty. In 1935 Chief Constable Captain A. F. Horden was largely responsible for implanting the first type of national police messaging service called Express Message. It was thanks to Express Message that the Northwich Safe Robbery was solved. 147 police headquarters and newspapers in London and Manchester were sent details about the robbery of £7,500 in notes and £150 of silver and copper. Six days later, the safe and all but £200 were recovered thanks to public information. Forensic science, such as it was, was used to examine the safe, and arrests were made.

In 1965, with Chief Constable H Watson at the helm, the Cheshire Constabulary arrested Ian Brady and Myra Hindley on 7th October after receiving a phone call from Hindley's brother-in-law about the murder of Edward Evans. Cheshire Police offices also led the search on Saddleworth Moor for the bodies of their victims - Pauline Reade, John Kilbride, Keith Bennet, Lesley Ann Downey and Edward Evans – all children aged between 10 and 17. Both Brady and Hindley maintained they were innocent of all charges but were both found guilty of the murders of Edward Evans, Lesley Ann Downey and John Kilbride in

1966, after the death penalty had been abolished on 8th November 1965.

In wasn't until 1985 that the full extent of their crimes was known as the pair finally confessed their guilt and Brady confessed to the murders of Pauline Reade and Keith Bennett.

The bodies of John Kilbride and Lesley Ann Downey were both found buried on Saddleworth Moor in 1965, which, along with evidence recovered from their home, led to the Moors Murders convictions. After the confessions of Brady to the press, the case of the Moors Murders was reopened, but it wasn't until 1987 that Pauline Reade's body was discovered. But Keith Bennett's body remains missing to this day.

Many searches have been launched by the police and even funded by public contributions to try and find the body, and though the police have once again closed the Moors Murders case, his family continue to search for his body. Both Hindley and Brady were jailed and died in prison. Hindley died in 2002 and Brady in 2017. The torture and murders that the pair committed earned Hindley the name of the most evil woman Britain and the trial judge, Mr Justice Fenton Atkinson described the pair as two sadistic killers of the utmost depravity. Both sentiments I am inclined to whole-heartedly agree with.

In 1984 the Cheshire Police helped to excavate the site where the Lindow Man, a mummified murder victim believed to be more than 1,500 years old. The body was discovered at a peat bog at Lindow Moss, just outside the town I grew up in. He had suffered a blow to the head, been garrotted and had his throat slit - clearly, someone didn't like him too much. Other remains have been found in the bog, so the Lindow Man is officially known as Lindow II.

In 1993, the Cheshire Police were faced with a number of terror attacks by the IRA. The first was an explosion at a gas depot in Warrington on the night that PC Mark Toker stopped a van for a routine stop check and was shot in the leg and back by the men involved with gas depot bombing. That was in February.

On 20th March 1993, when I was 6 years old (and it is sadly one of my earliest memories) two bombs went off in Warrington town centre. The town was packed with shoppers, 56 of whom were injured, and two children Tim Parry, 12, and Johnathan Ball, 3, were killed. Ball was with his babysitter shopping for a Mother's Day card and died at the scene. Parry did on 25th March in hospital. The Tim Parry - Johnathan Ball Foundation for Peace opened The Peace Centre in Warrington on 20th March 2000.

This was not an end to the terror threats in Cheshire, these were merely the first.

There have been many murders that the Cheshire Police have investigated, but few have attained the national exposure that the murder of teenager Shafilea Ahmed gained. Her murder was committed in 2003, but it wasn't until 2012 that her parents were found guilty of the "honour killing".

Though it may seem that in taking a brief snapshot of the

history of the Cheshire Constabulary it is filled with murder and terror, it is a tiny look at what police forces up and down the country have to deal with on a daily basis. From petty pilfering, anti-social behaviour, being cursed at and attacked, responding to domestic violence calls, drugs, rape, assault, burglary, murder and the abuse of children, the police are faced with the worst of humanity and the worst that humanity can do to one another on a daily basis. They are slated in the press and treated with disdain by many, yet they undertake dangerous work to protect the public. When reading through these crimes, I would ask you to think about what horrors I have omitted from their descriptions and perhaps have a little more appreciation for those that form the thin blue line.

The Devonshire Arms is a pub in Beeley, Derbyshire. It can be found in the grounds of Chatsworth House (one of the most beautiful country houses in England) and originally opened in 1747 when the three cottages that it had once been were converted into an inn. There were three inns in Beeley between 1755 and 1764, but only the Devonshire Arms has survived. It is still a pub that is open to the general public, and quaintly retains its 18th Century charm.

Wales and England have something of a turbulent history as neighbours, and aside from the brutality of England vs Wales rugby matches, there is a lot less animosity now than there has been in the past. However, in the 1830s things were not so bright. Arwyn wanting to leave Wales for England was not just a snub for his family but his country as well. The English thought of the Welsh as illiterate moral vacuums, something that has been underlined by the collection of Blue Books that were released 12 years ago and uploaded as part of the National Library of Wales Digital Mirror programme.

The Blue Books were commissioned in 1847 after a series of rather violent clashes made government officials feel that they needed to conduct a survey of Wales. In 1839, there were riots in Newport and Llanidloes and in the 1840s there were the Rebecca riots (though I won't go into details about those until we reach them in Stickleback Hollow's chronology) The main reason for the Blue Books conclusions about the Welsh were that most of the population didn't speak English and the view that "Teach English and bigotry will be banished" was the only answer that was shared by three of the Blue Books' authors.

This view is especially sad given that the 2001 census reported that only 20.8% of the population could speak the language, placing it on the UNs endangered languages list along with Scots Gaelic. The census revealed that 582,000 people in Wales, 100,000 Welsh speakers in England, Scotland and Northern Ireland and 25,000 Welsh speakers living in Patagonia, Argentina were all the Cymraeg or y Gymraeg speakers that remained. I can speak exactly one sentence in Welsh (I am a dragon).

Chartism was a movement that grew out of the discontent of workers across Britain. Chartism took its name from the People's Charter of 1838 that demanded votes for all men (yes, there was a time when not all men were allowed to vote – just like women) not just the gentry.

In Wales, the main centres of militant Chartism were in Newport, Newtown and Llanidloes. In Llanidloes, at the time, people were working in some of the most terrible conditions imaginable and were still cripplingly poor.

Discontent had increased in Wales during the 1830s and was made even worse during the economic depression of 1837-38. Llanidloes was one area where this was especially prevalent as there was a crisis in the flannel industry that was essential to the local economy (from 1797 a fortnightly flannel market was established at Welshpool and the flannel made in Llanidloes was piled onto a cart in bales of 120yds of flannel and taken to the market) The Poor Law Act of 1834 and the Corn Laws also had a horrible effect on the poverty that people in Llanidloes experienced.

Parliament were not keen to accept any word from groups that talked about workers' rights and the two Chartist petitions that were signed by a staggering number of supporters, which led some members to believe that the only way to accomplish change was through force. Others believed that peaceful reform through morality and justice was the way forward, so there was a difference in opinion on the best way to proceed within the movement.

Richard Jerman, a master carpenter, set up a branch of the Chartist movement in Llanidloes in 1838 and meetings were held around the town including in the Red Lion Inn on Long Bridge Street.

At the start of April 1839 a large but peaceful Chartist meeting was held and Henry Hetherington, a London Chartist and campaigner for free press, came to speak to people. Despite the peaceful nature of the meeting, rumours grew about an armed meeting happening later that month, which alarmed local magistrates. At the time, Llanidloes only had one elderly night watchman and some unpaid constables to keep law and order. So a request was made for constables from London to be sent to keep the peace in the town. Three constables were sent, and 300 men were recruited from the town to police the area.

Rather than ease tension in the area, the armed force of men roaming the streets in the name of law and order only served to worsen it.

On 30th April 1839, a Chartist meeting was held on the Long Bridge over the River Severn. During this meeting, word was brought that the three constables from London had arrested three Chartist supporters and that they were being held at the Trewythn Arms Hotel. The Chartists went to the Trewythn Arms only to discover that is was surrounded by fifty men, all armed with wooden staves.

The Chartists engaged the armed men and as a mob, stormed the hotel to rescue their friends. During the fray the interior of the hotel was left in ruins, one of the policemen was badly beaten whilst the other two escaped and went into hiding, fearing for their lives. But this was not the end of the trouble.

Until 4th May the town was peaceful as the Chartist patrols kept law and order in Llanidloes. But word had been sent to the Lord Lieutenant at Powis Castle about Chartist mobs roaming Llanidloes and the army had been dispatched to quell the riots.

It was Saturday 4th May 1839 when Infantrymen from Brecon

and Yeoman Cavalry numbering 200 strong came into the town with sabres drawn. They faced almost no resistance and the town was sealed off. Thirty Chartists, three of whom were women, were arrested and sent to Montgomery jail. A military garrison remained in the town until 1840. A £100 reward was offered for information about the whereabouts of Lewis Humphreys and Thomas Jerman after they were freed from the Trewythn Arms by the mob.

Five of the six demands made in the People's Charter of 1838 became part of the British constitution. The only one to be excluded was the demand for an annually elected Parliament.

The idea of a serial killer hadn't even entered the minds of the general populous in Victorian England. Jack the Ripper wouldn't hit headlines until 1888, and it wouldn't be until 1930 when the concept of a serial killer would even be considered. Ernst Gennat was the first man to use the word Serienmörder (serial murder). It was used to describe Peter Kürten. Kürten was also known as the Vampire of Dusseldorf who committed several murders and sexual assaults as well as a multitude of other crimes.

This isn't to say that there weren't serial killers throughout history. It is most likely that the legends of monsters, werewolves and vampires were created to explain away the actions of medieval serial killers. Periodically in Africa, there are outbreaks of murder that are committed by lion or leopard men. The Prince of Jidong in 144BC would go out and murder people with a gang of 20 to 30 men and seize their possessions for the fun of it. Then there are the cults that have killed thousands of people, including the Thuggee cult in India that is thought to have killed as many as one million people between 1740 and 1840.

The idea that serial murder for self-gratification did not fit with the model of an Englishman, something that can be seen in Doctor Hales attitude to the newspaper's suggestion of a killer murdering people to fit a nursery rhyme. The Victorian Englishman was expected to be protective of his wife, take pride in his work and practice good social behaviour with a stalwart moral fibre at his heart. He was expected to be courageous, patriotic and independent as well. None of this would allow for anything as callous or debasing as serial murder.

Envelopes have existed since around 3500 BC but rather than being made from paper, they were clay spheres that were moulded around coins and used in the Middle East for private transactions.

Paper envelopes were invented in China in 2 BC and are known as chih poh. They are used to store gifts or money and were used in the Southern Song Dynasty to give gifts of money to government officials.

In Europe, hand-made paper envelopes could be bought in 1838, but it wasn't until 1845 that a patent was granted in Britain for the first envelope making machine. It was given to Edwin Hill and Warren De La Rue. These envelopes were flat diamonds with folds so that they could be folded around a letter and then sealed. The folds could be held together by glue, paste or even a wax seal.

Mr Hunter waking up early on his own would have been a

matter of habit, something he couldn't break as the first mechanical alarm clock wasn't patented until 1847 by French inventor Antonie Redier. That isn't to say that alarm clocks didn't exist before that. Plato was said to have a large water clock that made the sound of a water organ when it went off and is thought to have been used to tell people when his lectures at dawn began. Ctesibius, the Hellenistic engineer also had a water clock that had a dial, pointer and an alarm system that "could be made to drop pebbles on a gong, or blow trumpets (by forcing bell-jars down into the water and taking the compressed air through a beating reed) at pre-set times."

There are also examples of water clocks being used as alarm clocks by the Romans and in China. Mechanical alarm clocks began to appear in the 15th Century in Europe where a pin was placed in a ring of holes around the clock dial at the appropriate time. In the 14th Century, some clock towers were able to chime at a fixed time each day. In 1787, Levi Hutchins, an American, made his own alarm clock, but it could only go off at 4am every day to wake him up for work.

By 1827, Strasbourg was known as the pâté de foie gras capital of the world, so it is not too much of a creative leap to see the dish in the pantry of a great house like Grangeback. Dried meats and salted meats were commonplace in Victorian times as they didn't have the modern conveniences of fridge freezers and deep-freeze units we have today - Electrolux didn't patent the first refrigerator until 1922. Pantries were cool and dark and helped to preserve food, and cold rooms existed in some places around the world. It is interesting to note that in 1850 the first demonstration of artificial refrigeration occurred, but it took 72 years until it became available for domestic use.

Biltong is not all that dissimilar to jerky - there are three differences between the two 1) Biltong tends to be thicker. 2) Biltong is dried with vinegar, salt and spices, traditionally jerky is only dried with salt. 3) Jerky is often smoked, but biltong never is - this aside, biltong is dried strips of meat and hails from South Africa. The Khoikhoi and other indigenous people preserved their meat by slicing it into strips, salting it and hanging it up to dry. When European settlers arrived in South Africa in the early 1600s, they added vinegar, saltpetre, pepper, coriander and cloves into the biltong drying process. As it existed for some many years and with British forces moving across the world, it is safe to assume that an old soldier such as Old Woakes would have developed a taste for it whilst campaigning.

Salford Central Railway station was opened on 29th May 1838 and was the terminus on the Manchester and Bolton Railway. It was originally named Salford Railway Station, but this was changed in 1988 when it became Salford Central to avoid confusion with Salford Crescent Station, which had been newly built. The station did stand on the opposite side of the road to New Baily Prison, with Upper Booth Street lying between the prison and the railway line, though you accessed the train station from Gore Street (instead of running across the train tracks)

Construction on the New Bailey Prison began on 22nd May 1787 when Thomas Butterworth Bayley laid the foundation stone. The prison was named after Mr Bayley and was closed in 1868 after Strangeways was built in 1866 and the prisoners were transferred there. Today the site of the prison is occupied by offices. The prison could be found in Salford on the banks of the River Irwell with Stanley Street between it and the water. The area around the prison was heavily industrialised, and an article from the Manchester Guardian in 1868 said "Between the felons' workshop and the boundary is a piece of ground where, some thirty years ago, vegetables grew abundantly, and the wall of the workshops bore a splendid crop of currants. But the chemical and other works in the neighbourhood and the exhalations of the river have changed all that, and nothing but rhubarb will grow there now." Women and men were housed in the same prison but in different sections. The women's section of the prison originally ran parallel to New Bailey Street, however by 1868; the prison was mainly used to house female prisoners, with most of the men occupying Strangeways.

Originally New Bailey prison was a square site with four arms radiating out from the centre surrounded by Falkner Street, Stanley Street, Bayley Street and Booth Street. However, by 1820 it had been extended so that it dwarfed the original site. You can see New Bailey Prison on the 1842 Ordinance Survey map here for digital readers or for

paperback readers at
https://maps.nls.uk/view/102344087#zoom=6&lat=5309&lon=5718&layers=BT
Unfortunately, I couldn't use the image itself as the maps are not licensed for commercial use. The slightly wonky black cross close to New Bailey Street is the original prison so you can see how much it grew since it was built.

http://manchesterhistory.net/manchester/gone/newbailey.html also has images of the prison from when it was built to what stands there now along with some plans of the prison from its small beginning to its final face before closure.

William Hughes was in charge of the Mitre Inn by 1840, though I am not sure when it passed from William Lloyd to William Hughes, the passing of the pub from one man to the other seemed to fit well in the narrative of this story.

Chester Racecourse lies on the banks of the River Dee and is built on the site of a Roman harbour. The racecourse is known as Roodee, which means the Island of the Cross, which comes from the raised mound at the centre of the field that is decorated by a small cross. It is said that the cross marks the burial site of a statue of the Virgin Mary that caused the death of Lady Trawst. The statue was tried and found guilty of murder by a jury of 12 men and sentenced to hang. Because it was sacrilege to hang the statue, it was left on the banks of the river, and the tide carried it downriver to Chester. If this story is true, it not only is one of the strangest tales of murder, it is also the first recorded case of a jury ever being used in a court.

In terms of horse racing, the first grandstand at the racecourse was finished in 1817, and the first recorded race was held on 9th February 1539. However, the first admittance fee wasn't recorded until 1897. For the doctor, Edryd and Derwyn's trip to the races, it is likely that they were attending the May Festival that was first introduced in 1766.

About the Series

Mysteries abound

When her parents die from fever, Lady Sarah Montgomery Baird Watson-Wentworth has to leave India, a land she was born and raised in, and travel to England for the first time. Finding it almost impossible to adjust to London society, Sarah flees to the county of Cheshire and the country estate of Grangeback that borders the village of Stickleback Hollow. A place filled with oddballs, eccentrics and more suspicious characters than you can shake a stick at, Sarah feels more at home in the sleepy little village than she ever did in the big city, however, even sleepy little villages have mysteries that must be solved.

Set in Victorian England, the Mysteries of Stickleback Hollow follows the crime solving efforts of Constable Arwyn Evans, Mr. Alexander Hunter and Lady Sarah Montgomery Baird Watson-Wentworth. From theft to murder, supernatural occurrences and missing people, Stickleback Hollow is a magical place filled with oddballs, outcasts, rogues, eccentrics and ragamuffins.

Preview from the next book

What Became of Henry Cartwright?

The countess sat in her room in shock. She had always known that the duchess was a ruthless woman, but had never fully understood what lengths she was prepared to go to or what her driving motivations were.

It was true that many men and women professed to doing all that they did for the glory of the empire, but it these words often rang hollow, especially when their actions proved to be solely self-serving.

But Lady de Mandeville had no way of knowing that Szonja was in the hall, listening to everything that was going on in the room, watching through the keyhole. The only person that she was talking to was a man that she had killed.

There was no reason for her to lie to a dead man or to even explain to him why he had to die. Yet, she had taken the time to explain what fate awaited the young man and why he was such a fool to cross her.

The countess had always disliked the duchess, not merely because she was a strong woman who succeeded in the world of business, but because she had always imagined that the duchess sought more power for herself.

This revelation of such selfless intentions, though accompanied by delusions of grandeur, were enough to give Szonja pause to not only consider her purpose for being on the estate, but her whole opposition to Lady de Mandeville and her plans.

She sat by the window and looked out at the grounds as she became lost in thought. The countess was so consumed by her thoughts that she didn't hear the footsteps approaching her room or the door to it being opened.

The first thing she knew of another being present in her room was the dull thud of something being placed firmly on her dressing table.

"Lady de Mandeville, I'm sorry, I didn't hear you come in," the countess stammered as her heart fluttered in her chest. The sound of a heavy box being placed on her dressing table had startled her, but the presence of her hostess was far more terrifying, especially after what she had just witnessed.

"You seemed to be contemplating something important, though this may be somewhat more important to you," the duchess said coolly as she uncovered the box.

"And what is this?" Szonja asked innocently.

"Every keyhole has an eye and every wall ears. My maid told me that you were stood outside my study just now. Please do not waste any time by trying to deny it. You were sent here to spy on me, something that I am sure you took great pleasure at being asked to do. What you overheard in my study may warrant some explanation," Carol-Ann said brusquely,

"And what explanation is it that you care to give me?" the countess asked as she peered curiously at the box.

"This box contains everything that the late Lord St. Vincent was trying to use as blackmail leverage. If you wish to read all contained within, you will be in the same position that he was. You have seen what happens to those who try to blackmail me and you heard the motivations of my blackmailer. Though we have always been on opposite sides, this may help you understand my position better, and why what I have done has been done for the good of the Empire,"

Lady de Mandeville said as she turned on her heel and left the countess alone with the box.

Szonja waited until the duchess had gone and the door to her room was firmly closed before she rose to examine the chest. It seemed strange to her that something that was clearly damning for Lady de Mandeville should be so readily offered to her.

She understood the duchess' threat of death well enough, but in England there were limits as to what Lady de Mandeville could do to the Countess of Huntingdon.

As long as Szonja kept what she learned to herself whilst she was in India, she was not in any immediate danger.

Though she didn't understand the logic of the duchess, she was curious as to what kind of information the chest contained. To have such power over a woman like Lady de Mandeville, the countess could only imagine how terrible the secrets were.

She picked up the first of the papers and began to read. As she read, her brow became furrowed. She moved onto the next paper and the next. The more she read, the more she understood what actions the duchess had taken in the East to secure the hold of the Empire not only for trade, but a stable occupation that benefited the British people and those that had submitted to British rule.

It wasn't just India that this applied to, but the rest of the Empire as well. Every corner that the British had conquered and named as a colony was secured through the actions that Lady de Mandeville had laid down, at least in the political and civil spheres.

By the time the countess had finished reading all the documents, she understood the duchess' reasoning for letting her read the documents. She folded each one back up and replaced them in the box.

There were many rumours about the Company and of the activities of John Smith, but reading through the files in the box made all of them seem to be nothing but opposition propaganda.

The countess sat for a while, thinking of all the things she had been told, everything she thought she knew of the duchess and everything she now knew.

It was now very clear why Lady de Mandeville had gone to such great lengths to procure the key that Mr. Hunter had found in the pocket watch that Lady Sarah's parents had stolen.

But it raised some rather alarming questions in the countess' mind.

Who had Colonel Montgomery Baird and Lady Watson-Wentworth been working for when they stole the pocket watch? If they knew that they were going to die, why had they risked the life of their daughter to bring the pocket watch to England? And why had Lady de Mandeville been unable to retrieve the pocket watch before it had left India with Lady Sarah?

Grab you copy now!

About the Author

I was born in Macclesfield, Cheshire, UK, and raised in the nearby town of Wilmslow. From an early age I discovered I had a flair and passion for writing.

I began writing at the age of 7 and was first published in 2010. I currently live with my partner, Matt, and our two cats in Christchurch, New Zealand.

As an avid horsewoman and gamer, I also have a passion for singing, dancing, the theatre, and my garden.

Facebook: https://www.facebook.com/AuthorC.S.Woolley

Instagram: https://www.instagram.com/thecswoolley

Website: http://.mightierthantheswordUK.com

Acknowledgements

Writing can be an extremely lonely profession at times, but thankfully I never have to go through any of the pressures alone. My wonderful Matthew has been a source of constant support to me during all of my writing endeavours since we first met. I couldn't ask for a more fitting partner to share my life or love with.

Writing is not something I stumbled into either, my mother, Helen, took me, and my sisters, to the library every weekend when we were young to get different books, and I always maxed out the number of books I could get. Not only did she encourage me to read, but to write as well. To say I have been writing stories and poetry since I was 7 is not an exaggeration and the development of my writing career is due in no small part to her.

My mother-in-law, Lesley, has also been a source of unflinching and unwavering support, something I could not do without.

To Laura and Sam, who have read and offered opinions, death threats and encouragement on my early drafts, you are true treasures. Amy, you too are worth your weight and more in gold for all your love and support.

It may seem that writers only function alone, but I am blessed to be part of an amazing community of authors whom I know that I have helped push me to even greater heights and success. So to Quinn Ward, Donna Higton, Charlene Perry, Scarlett Braden Moss, Bryan Cohen, Chez Churton, Eliza Green, John Beresford, Rich Cook, Robert Scanlon, Jen Lassalle, Cathy MacRae, Ariella Zoella, and Helen Blenkinsop, my dear friends, thank you.

And finally, to you, dear reader, without you there would be no books, no series, no career. I want to thank you for all the time that you spend reading my work, reviewing it, sharing it with your friends and family. Without you there would be nothing. Thank you from the bottom of my heart.

Until we meet again in my next book, thank you and adieu.

Made in the USA
Monee, IL
20 June 2022